death by zamboni

a true story

by David David Katzman

BEDHEAD BOOKS

A Bedhead Book
Published by Bedhead Books
bedheadbooks@yahoo.com
Chicago, IL
60657

ISBN : 0-615-11357-5
Library of Congress Card Number: 00-190732

Printed In the United States by Bang Printing

Cover Art by Shag
Book Design by Rob Brown
Photograph on back cover by Johanna Jacobson

this book is dedicated to everyone who ever dreamed of Justice.

death by zamboni

CHAPTER

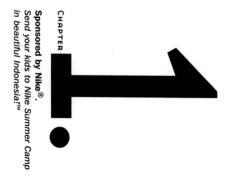

MY NAME IS SATAN DONUT. I'm a private investigator, and I've got an important story to tell. A story that needs to be heard. A story of significance. A story that's worth at least twenty dollars in hardback and twelve in paperback.

I remember when it all started. I was sitting at my desk waiting for time to pass.

It's a long wait.

How does that song go? "Time keeps on spinnin', spinnin', spinnin'...into the future." Man, I hate that song.

Time is our mortal enemy because it makes us mortal. Yet without time we wouldn't exist. And it would be damn hard to figure out what's on TV. Two-minute eggs would be right out.

Like lemmings at cliff edge, beads of sweat hurled themselves off my forehead onto my gunmetal-grey ink blotter. I was itching for a case. No, scratch that, it was my crabs acting up in the heat. What I really needed was an unguent of some kind. The only problem, gentle reader – and I'm assuming here you're still reading – is that unguents and heat don't mix. Neither do crabs and heat. No matter how you slice 'em. You can't even parboil 'em. And believe me, I've tried, Oh Lordy, how I've tried. And this particular day in question was hot. Damn hot. The kind of heat that causes H_2 to divorce 0, and Hall to break up with Oates. Which is really too bad for Oates because "Hall" is fine by itself. "Ladies and gentlemen, here's Hall!" That's okay. "Here's Oates?" That's just weird.

I was staring out my window, munching on a veggie burger, and having a cup of coffee to help me relax. The sun slapped against my window like a backhand to the right cheek. Like a brick across the ol' bean. When a brick sailed through my window sending glass shards across the room at Warp Factor

Three, Mr. Sulu, and landed square on my mung bean plant, all I could think was, "How ironic."

The dirt from my mung bean plant was strewn onto the hardwood floor in a pattern not unlike the Afro of Gabe Kaplan in the early episodes of "Welcome Back Kotter." Although, come to think of it, did his hair actually evolve as the show went on? Was it different in the later episodes? Frankly, I can't enjoy a sitcom if the characters' hairstyles don't grow with us as we get to know and love them. So much for Mr. Kotter as one of my role models.

I knelt by the dirt, uneasy with the ramifications of this symbolic representation of a traditionally "black" descriptive (i.e. the "Afro") applied to a white man. It reminded me of Elvis' appropriation of black music for his own success. I also reminded myself never to use a Latin derived abbreviation (i.e. i.e.) again. I rearranged the dirt until it looked more or less like the nose of former Minority Whip Dick Gephardt. This put me at ease.

I picked up the brick and peeled off the plant plastered on it like Wile E. Coyote under a boulder. I tossed the plant into the garbage with a snarl: I'd been growing that mung bean plant with intent to torture it later. I'm a vegetarian, you see, not because I love animals but because I hate plants. My antipathy developed in childhood when a rosebush started growing out of my hip. The kids used to call me "Rosehips." It's been a thorn in my side ever since.

I examined the brick closely. It looked much like a regular brick. There were several white paint marks on it in the shape of fingerprints. I studied these white marks for several minutes before I realized there was a note tied to the brick. I untied the pink bow and read the attached paper:

Hmmh. If only I'd gotten the message sooner...

Before I had a chance to ponder this delivery, there was a knock at my door. "One moment," I yelled, "I'm masturbating."

I wasn't, but I like to keep 'em guessing.

I quickly swept up the dirt and hid the brick in my hamper. I moved to the door like a cat in heat, arching my back, hissing and urinating on the hardwood floor. I opened the door and before my eyes I saw a wall, a box of Tic-Tacs®, Papa Smurf, God, stars, fame and fortune and everything that goes with it. Oops, that was the closet.

I went to the office door and pried it open with a crowbar to reveal a woman whose proportions could only be calculated with imaginary numbers. A rhapsody in blonde. Looking at her was an aerobic workout. Her face was so beautiful, it was like beauty squared. In fact, her face *was* square. She was the most gorgeous blockhead I'd ever seen.

In she walked.

Can you say Eeeeeyowchamamahahawawawawallawalla-boomboomayecarumba? Well, if you can, I'm impressed, but that and ten bucks'll get you a cup of coffee. She was blonder than blonde and sweeter than something really sweet.

What's the sweetest thing you can imagine? Visualize it right now. I'll give you a second.

Now, imagine eating it. Eat some more. Stuff yourself. Gorge upon it. Pound upon pound. Now get a garbage bag and vomit your lungs out. 'Til you've got the dry heaves. Now try to sniff a piece of that sweet stuff. Oh, no – vomiting again. Now you'll never be able to enjoy it. Too bad. Well, my point is that she's not quite as sweet as that and obviously smarter than you are.

As she stood there, hands on hips, her perfume floated to my nostrils – a tender yet inquisitive scent with a citrus foreground interweaving hints of heather, rose and Elmer's® Glue.

Remember when you were a kid letting Elmer's® Glue dry on your fingertips or making hand casts out of Elmer's® and then peeling them off? Remember trying to plug your butthole with Elmer's® because you were afraid the Four Horsemen of the Apocalypse were going to come riding out of your rear and the world was going to end? Don't worry, we've all done that at one time or another. Her perfume reminded me of those times.

The woman at my door wasn't so much voluptuous as... well... now that I think about it, she was voluptuous.

She whispered something.

"What?" I asked.

She pulled out a megaphone and repeated, "I SAID, 'SOMETHING.'"

"Oh."

She continued using the megaphone, producing the loudest whisper I've ever heard, "YOU'RE SATAN DONUT, RIGHT?"

"Yeah."

She sauntered saucily toward me but slipped and fell in the puddle of urine I had left on the floor, dropping her megaphone. As I helped her up, I apologized, "Sorry about that. Vomit from my drinking binge last night."

Keep 'em guessing.

She turned to face me and sat down on the edge of my desk. Then she laid back across the desk, smashed my desk lamp, flattened the Styrofoam cup of coffee, and utterly crushed my extensive collection of rare Russian wooden dolls that I happen to keep in a row on the edge of my desk. You know, the kind of dolls that fit one inside the other? Whatever the hell they're called. The coffee was partially absorbed by her dress but most dripped onto the floor. As she relaxed there on my desk, she brought her foot up and ground her stiletto heel into my veggie burger.

She called out to me, "I'm going to get right to the point. You're a dick for hire, and I need a dick."

"Hey," I snapped, "You can't talk to me like I'm some kind of two bit whore."

"I'm sorry," she said, "I thought I was using proper terminology. I need you to find my missing husband. And I'll have sex with you if you succeed."

"Well, that's different. I'll take the case."

She lay there on my desk for a bit as I idly watched a fly buzzing near the ceiling light. Finally she spoke, "Do you want me to explain the situation?"

I turned my back and pondered the question. "Only if you feel it will help me solve the case."

"Okay, my name is..." she began but was interrupted when my phone rang.

I held up a hand. "Excuse me for a second. This might be my V.D. report."

I answered the phone, "Hello. Satan Donut."

"Yeah, dude. It's Moe Ped."

"Who?"

"Dude. I got a hot shipment in."

"What?"

"Listen! This is seriously good shit."

"Ah."

"I can get you some... shrimp... if you catch my meaning."

"What kind of shrimp?" I decided to play along. Looks like someone had dialed a wrong number, and a drug deal had fallen into my lap. I could use some extra drugs.

"We got mauve shrimp and shrimp ala carte...know what I'm sayin'?"

"How mauve is mauve?"

"I'm talkin' Power Ranger Mauve. We'll bake a cake for you, half price for a box. I'm talking under wholesale here for seventeen untraceable kilos of tracing paper, if you read my drift."

"Got any tickets to the Phish concert?" I asked. "I could use three."

"Gotcha covered. Three ankle weights coming right up, my dog. We'll be by later. Ciao."

I hung up.

"Well, what were the results?" she inquired kindly as she settled herself more comfortably onto my desk.

"Of what?"

"Your V.D. report."

"Not to worry. They were positive, very positive."

She continued, "As I was saying, my name is..." This time she was interrupted by a buzzing sound from my pants.

As I removed my Pocket E-Mail Pal® from my pocket, I said, "Hold on another second. This might be my proctologist." I unfolded the collapsible keyboard and downloaded my email using the built in cellular hook-up. It was an email from my sister.

To: Ratat@calm.com (Satan Donut)
From: Joydivision@dot.com (Etta Donut)
Subject: Kill corporations

Another day doing the evil temp grind. Will wonders never cease? I'm at this ad agency called Feet, Clone & Bendover working for this anal cunt in charge of research for Procter & Gamble. She mentioned casually that I should wear makeup and I'd look more presentable. Who the fuck are these bougoeis (?) pigs to judge me? Think about this - HITLER was good at his job. I was pretty ticked off so I rigged her mouse to give her an "accidental" 300 volt charge. If she doesn't die she sure will have a killer perm tomorrow morning.

I've got practice tonight and Spitto better not be on the Redrum shit again or I'll jam my combat boot right up his ass. Goddammit I wish we could find a new drummer but man, drummers are hard to come by.

I wrote a new song on my lunch break called Anxiety. What do you think?

Anxiety drives me mad,
Like shitting rusty nails,
Like getting your hand caught in a bear trap —
Do you have the guts to let it go?
And how do you sever it if you have no medical experience?
Do you slowly saw the veins then tendons then bone?
Or do you take hacks at the hand awkwardly?
How do you stop the bleeding once it's removed?
Can I bleed neatly? That's bloody neat. Look at that hand.
That Darn Hand starring Marlo Thomas as the severed hand.
Slavery drip-drool of a cock sliced lengthwise.
Add cheeze-whiz and presto!
A cheese cock! Munch heartily.
How do you run from yourself?
Our very being-ness holds us tight, compressed,
caught like a cornered rat with bleeding sores on its lips,
Anxiously gnawing it's own pus-y, lipstick red sores.
(repeat end)

My darling sister. Issues? Sure. That girl needs a magazine rack to hold all her issues. "Sorry, I'll just be a moment," I explained to the woman in my office as I began typing my response.

To: Joydivision@dot.com (Etta Donut)
From: Ratat@calm.com (Satan Donut)
Subject: Dun's Inane Hill

Dear Etta,

It's good to hear from you. I hope your new job goes well. Sounds like you've made many new friends right off the bat. I just hope it's better than your last job that I believe you said sucked like a black hole in your anus. But I could be mistaken. Maybe you said you loved it like a good salad.

Things are going well here. I just landed a new case from this cubic-headed woman. I'm still having my bed-wetting problem despite the electroshock therapy.

Right soon.

Love,
Satan

I fired off the email and returned to my potential client. "Thanks for waiting. You were saying?"

"How was the report?" she asked.

"What?"

"The proctologist report," she explained pointing at her rear.

"He said I was fine, but I need to keep my eyes peeled for boils."

"That sounds like good news," she commented. "So, where was I? My name is..." Again the phone rang.

"Una momento, por favor."

I answered, "Hola."

"Satan."

"Hi, Mom."

"It's your mother."

"Yes."

"Your father's on the other line."

Silence, then she screamed, "HEY BIG DADDY!!!" right into the phone. There was a scrambling as he picked up the line.

"Right here kiddo. Howdy doo there my sweet babushka," said my father.

"Dad."

"We need to ask you something important," said my mom.

"Uh-huh."

"Have you... seen... *Cats* yet?" asked my mother.

"No."

"Oh, you really should next time it comes around," Mom said. "I like the music because it's jazzy, but the costumes...and the staging! It was all written by that poet, you know."

"Which poet?" asked my dad.

"Oh...shut-up," retorted Mom.

"You mean T.S. Eliot?" said Dad.

"Yes. Now shut up."

"Your mother always forgets. But the costumes and staging is marvelous."

My mother explained, "I could remember all the characters and the plot, and I'll forget the author or title. Your dad has some sweaters you might want to look at. Mt. Everest sweaters."

"Mmmh," I replied.

"Sir Edmund Hillary wore the same kind."

"Uh huh."

"He climbed Mt. Everest," stated my mom.

"Wasn't it Mt. Fujimoto?" asked Dad.

"Oh, shut up, you," she rejoined.

"Uh huh," I repeated.

"He did," emphasized my mother.

"Mmmh. I gotta go now."

"All right. Don't forget your socks, especially if you're going to Egypt."

I hung up. Then, turning to the woman lying prone on my desk and staring at the ceiling, I said, "Please proceed."

"My name is Vagina Dentata, and my husband is Bland Entropy," she explained. "You've surely heard of him? World-renowned philanthropist and biochemist. His theories of bio-chemistry have revolutionized the world of biochemistry."

"How long have you been married?" I asked.

"One year give or take a year," she replied.

"And you decided not to take his last name?"

"No. I really wanted him to have it. We had two children who are now 16 and 18 years old, Miranda and Igor."

"Respectively?" I inquired.

"I don't respect them at all."

"Right."

"We live in a mansion in Nicetown with two servants: our butler and maid. Igor has a pet werewolf, and Bland has a laboratory assistant who used to live with us, but she disappeared the same time he did."

"Very suspicious," I mused aloud. Perhaps their disappearances were somehow...connected.

I stood thoughtfully staring out my shattered window at the kids playing on the street below. They were playing catch with a friendly old lady. The old lady, however, didn't seem to like being thrown around. On second thought, they were probably beating up the old lady.

"How long has he been missing?" I asked.

"About a month."

"What did the police say?"

"Nothing. I forgot to tell them."

"Mmh. What can you tell me about the day he disappeared?"

"I was in Paris at the time having an affair with a French Poodle."

"Really?" I asked, raising an eyebrow, "you actually like the French?"

"The French aren't nearly as bad as they want you to think they are. Bland and I had an open relationship. I was open for business, and he could deal with it."

"Very good. Why did you finally decide to look for him?"
I asked.

"Well, I can't inherit his family fortune until he's found
dead. Or, if he's alive, I want to know how long he has left
to live."

"Fine. I think that's enough information for now."

Vagina turned on her side, her dress dripping with coffee,
shards of doll jabbing into her side. "I could pay you right
now for finding my husband if you want, right on your desk."

"No thanks. I've got a bad case of blue balls from dry hump-
ing a crash test dummy this afternoon."

"I could suck you off," she offered.

"Gives me hives."

She got up sensuously from the desk, her large breasts
spilling out of her dress and onto the floor.

"Please find my husband, Mr. Donut," she continued. "My
credit rating depends on it."

"I'm the man for the job," I asserted. "I think I'll start by
questioning your children."

"They just went bowling. You can find them at the Cannabis Bowl."

"How will I recognize them?"

"You can't miss Igor. He's got a cauliflower ear and the heart of an artichoke." She got up, leaving a big wet spot on my desk blotter, and sauntered to the door before turning her sexy cubic head back to look at me.

"You look smaller...from here."

Then she left.

Well, I thought...well, well, well. Well. Great. Well.

A missing guy. And there are how many places in this world to hide a guy? A billion. No way. More. More than a trillion. Imagine that. That's a lot of hiding places. I was going to have to get an early start.

This case definitely had a mysterious side to it. There's this guy. And he's missing. Nobody knows where he is. His whereabouts are a mystery. Hence "mysterious."

I smelled danger, so I decided to pack some serious artillery. While working on my last case – The Case of the Juggler's Jugular – I unfortunately allowed myself to be dangerously unprepared. I was in a bathroom stall taking a dump when I was surrounded by two Doberman Pinchers, four gang-bangers, five dirty cops, six ninja assassins, twenty members of the Mormon Tabernacle Choir and a partridge in a pear tree. All trying to kill me. The only weapons I had on hand were a rubber band and a Pez® dispenser. Fortunately, I'm a master of Pez® Fu, but it was still a tough fight for the first twenty-two minutes.

This time I wasn't going to get caught with my pants down. I packed two 10mm automatics, a Magnum .45, a Howitzer with Agent Orange canisters, and an iM1A2 Abrams Tank. I also packed my go-to weapon, the Spud Gun.

Just as I was about to leave there was another knock at my door. I opened it, and there was some guy in a delivery uniform with a wheelbarrow. He handed me a clipboard, pointed to a spot, "Sign here."

As I looked at the form, he wheeled the wheelbarrow into my office. "Where do you want it?"

"What the hell is this stuff?"

He gestured at the clipboard, "It says right there – three bike tires, a rusty fork and 17 boxes of Brillo Pads."

"What the hell?!?"

"You ordered from Mr. Ped, right?

"Well, yeah, but…"

"Didya' order or not?"

"Yeah, yeah." Damnit. I thought I was using proper terminology.

"So where do you want it?"

"Dump it in the closet."

To: Ratat@calm.com (Satan Donut)
From: Joydivision@dot.com (Etta Donut)
Subject: Eat shit, and additionally, die

Well, my boss never touched the mouse pad.
Unfortunately, the cleaning lady went in at five to dust
and got fried by my booby trap. It's sad when the pro-
letariat are caught in the battle between the radicals
and the capitalist class but the training wheels of the
revolution will occasionally be greased with the blood
of the innocent.

Do you ever get that existentialist depression? That
feeling that since you can't define your "self" that

life is meaningless? That we are all worthless, dirty and it would be better to be dead than to have to keep your body alive? That your mind is constantly torturing you with horrible thoughts you can't escape? And no one in the world can be trusted, and inevitably they will find out you're a fraud and a phony?

Well, be happy if you do, because those are my good days. On days like today when the thoughts come to life like cobras spitting poison, I find a storage closet and strike my head repeatedly with a ballpeen hammer. So far, that has distracted me from killing myself.

The whore I work for asked me to get coffee for her and some client who was in her office. I'm sorry. That's an insult to all the whores in the world. I apologize whores. So I pissed in the coffee.

I think there should be a Swastika key on the keyboard. It seems like a natural. Perhaps it could replace the dollar sign. It would really simplify things. Instead of putting one's name at the end of a memo, one could just put a Swastika. It could even replace the company logo. Hell, instead of actually writing anything in these memos, people could just type row after row of Swastikas.

Anyways I wrote another song called Dog Shit

Watching a wealthy woman in the park with her dog.
The dog squats, shits, strains.
Squats, shits, strains.
The woman stands, stares, ignores and moves on.
Stands, stares, ignores.
I see the puddle and stain she leaves behind.
Glistening puddle, I roll in the puddle.
Oh Poodle of Doom, you have wrought my fate in your
shit.
You shit my life in gasping strains.
Nice leather coat, ma'am, nice lipstick.
Would you like me to slaughter Jews?
And blacks, too?
Oh, have I gone too far for you pretty bitch?
Let's just earn more money and let the boss do
the talking.

To: Joydivision@dot.com (Etta Donut)
From: Ratat@calm.com (Satan Donut)
Subject: Inner piece is a gun in the pocket

Since there is no point to life, there is no point in
working, and there is no point in not working. There is

no point in killing yourself, and there is no point in not killing yourself. There is no point in continuing this sentence, but there is also no point in not continuing this sentence. You see my point?

I've got a book you need to read. It's called "The Idiot's Guide To Capitalism." You can also borrow my other equally informative books: "The Idiot's Guide To Being an Idiot," "The Idiot's Guide To The Idiot's Guide To Being An Idiot," and "The Idiot's Guide To Ass Fucking." I think it would help you through this difficult period of confronting the nature of capitalism. Yes, capitalism has no mercy, has not pity, feels no pain. Capitalism is not a guy I want to have a beer with or join at Parcheesi. Capitalism is not hygienic and does not clean under his fingernails. Trying to get on Capitalism's good side is like trying to talk back to a backless dress. I've tried it, and it only results in a flying hook kick to the privates.

Yes, I know all this and more. At least, I used to know more. Now that my long-term memory is shot, I can only leave it to the younger kids like you to right everything my generation has fucked up. And all the generations before mine fucked up. And the dinosaurs fucked up. And the aliens.

Have a few beers. You'll be fine.
—Chairman e-Mao

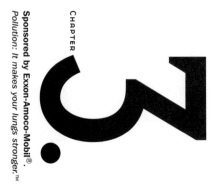

CHAPTER

I took the rickety elevator down to the ground level and exited the beat-up front door to the steps. The croak of frogs. The smell of eucalyptus. A crocodile roar. A gentle breeze. Ah, the Louisiana Bayou. Too bad I'm in Chicago. A chill breeze hit me like a divorce settlement. Sure, it was 95° an hour ago, but Chicago weather is extremely unpredictable.

No time to waste, I jumped on my hog and rode right to the Cannabis Bowl. I used to hang out there all the time when I was playing "Shooting at Bowlers for Dollars." I pushed my way through the entry doors and went up to the counter.

There was an ancient man working the register. He was wizened, as they say, like a prune. He had lost all his hair and even the top of his head was wrinkled. His head had so many grooves, it looked like one of those maze games in a box where you roll a ball by twiddling the knobs and try not to let it drop into a hole. But the thing is, it always falls into a hole.

I love these old timers. They've always got hundreds of stories to tell, each more outrageous than the next. He jutted his veiny neck forward like a box turtle, pointing at me with a small, pointy nose, and grunted "Hello" with a toothless mouth, and then he died. Just fell to the ground lifeless.

I tried desperately to reach over the counter to snag a pair of size elevens, but I couldn't reach them. Eventually, I had to climb over the counter to grab one. I found a nice pair – one side green, the other red. They went well with my complexion.

Igor and Miranda were in Lane 1. He was easily recognized by the large white cauliflower on the side of his head. It looked heavy enough to throw off his balance, but perhaps he'd learned to compensate.

There was a married couple with three kids using Lane 2, so I surreptitiously showed them my first place trophy for Bowler Shooting, and they cleared out quickly. I observed Igor and Miranda from this vantage. I noted that the side wall of the bowling alley was partly knocked down, and there was a construction crew working on the building. There were various exposed electrical wires, steel girders, and, every once in a while, a wrecking ball would swing by. Nobody seemed to mind. When you gotta bowl, you gotta bowl. Once, I saw a guy refuse to interrupt a perfect game even when his wife and kids were carried off by a giant Sasquatch. I had my personal high score during an earthquake.

Igor made a spare, and as he returned to the scoring station Miranda said, "Nice shot. Down to the wire." She took her ball and stood holding it, staring at the pins. She concentrated for ten minutes. Tension mounted. Then Igor mounted a tension wire. Miranda stood utterly still as Igor threaded his penis through a loop in the wire, and blue electricity coursed around his body like a force field. Finally, in an ecstatic burst, his semen – buzzing with blue electricity – fired from his penis, sailed across five lanes, and landed in the mouth of a fat, bearded, Bowling League of Kiwanis captain. The captain's head glowed blue and then promptly exploded.

"Nice shot," intoned Miranda then bowled a strike to win. They began collecting their belongings as I bowled twenty quick gutterballs in a row to finish my game before racing to catch them on the way out.

"Are you Miranda and Igor Bland?" I inquired.

"Hold on," said Miranda as they checked their nametags, "Yes."

"Right. My name is Satan Donut," I stated while showing them my P.I. ID.

"What's PI stand for?" Igor asked, looking at my ID.

"Approximately 3.14159265," I answered.

"Oh," he stated.

"Your mother hired me to find your father," I disclosed.

"Oh. Why?" Miranda wondered.

"He's missing," I explained.

"Oh...What's he missing?" she queried.

"Clearly the ability to have intelligent children," I replied.

"Oh. Sounds awful," Igor commented.

"Trust me, it really is," I riposted. "So I take it you didn't notice anything different the day he disappeared?"

"I didn't even notice he was gone," she clarified.

"You guys have been a great help," I told them.

"Super!" Igor exclaimed.

"Why don't I head back with you to your house?" I suggested.

"Okey-doke," she responded.

We walked out to their car. I'd leave my hog at the bowling alley. No one would fuck with him. I ride a 2000 pound pure-bred Barrow Pig named Rush. As far as I know, it's the largest pig in the world. People think pigs are slow, but that's just a common misconception. At a gallop, Rush can reach up to sixty miles per hour. Another common misconception is that pigs are stupid. I think the only thing holding them back is their lack of hands. If pigs had hands, they'd rule this planet.

Miranda's car was a mini-hearse. It has the practicality of a mini-van and the handy carrying capacity of a hearse combined. If you get annoyed with your kids at soccer practice, you can always kill them on the way home and take them directly to the cemetery. I squeezed in between Miranda and Igor in the front seat. Miranda gunned the engine and backed out of the parking space. We took Lake Shore Drive east to 390 and then headed west toward Nicetown.

I picked up a couple sheets of newspaper lying under my feet and tried to read them. Unfortunately, they were covered in mud, and I could only make out part of one article that read, "Be on the lookout for land mimes. Mimes are finally getting revenge for all the abuse they've taken over the years. The public has been warned to avoid subway stops where the mimes can be found terrorizing the innocent by trapping them in invisible boxes, blowing them into walls with big fans, and squirting them with fake flowers filled with hydrochloric acid." I rolled the paper up and tucked it away, possibly as evidence. I occupied myself for the remainder of the trip playing pocket pool.

We exited at Nicetown and passed a sign which read:

WELCOME TO NICETOWN
pop. 4,23〜
Hey! Quit shoving my arm!

We took a right on Biggley Boulevard, and I studied the houses as we passed them. A brown raised ranch, a brick single flat, a white colonial, an igloo, an adobe hut, a nudist colony, a demonic castle rising one thousand feet into the air surrounded by dark clouds shooting lightning and vultures circling overhead, a couple of gray stone townhomes, etc.

Miranda pulled over to the side of the road where an old woman stood clutching a rubber chicken. Igor rolled down his window, and Miranda yelled across us, "Hello Grandma Fred, what's going on?" I noticed a crowd behind her gathered between two houses. There were several police cars parked in the driveways.

"Whatcha doin', Grandma?" asked Miranda again.

"I was hopin' to catch a lift home, but it looks like you guys are heading out," she answered.

"What do you mean?" asked Miranda.

"Well, you just passed our house," replied Grandma Fred.

"Oh, right. Which one is it again?"

"The big black castle with the vultures."

"Oh," said Miranda. "Well, we're going back. You want a ride?"

"Why the fuck not?"

There was no room in the front seat so Grandma Fred climbed into the back and lay down.

"What's going on over there?" I asked her, gesturing at the crowd on the lawn.

"Well, homeslice," she said, "if you look closely in the grass by that house over there you can see what at first glance might appear to be a pile of dirty laundry, but if you go up there you'll see it's actually a bloody stabbed body. Hoo-hah. He was stabbed seventy-two times in the shape of a smiley face."

"The victim," she continued, "one Jan-Erik Everyman, was a terminally ill sado-masochist who always wanted to exit life as a bloody heap. Looks like he got his wish. There were witnesses to the crime who claim Jan-Erik cried for joy when Minister Meateater stabbed him with a seven-inch Henkles carving knife.

"It was merely a fortuitous accident, really," she went on. "The Minister believed he was icing his five year old grandson's birthday cake, but he can't see so good up close.

"Mind you, Minister Meateater can pick off a sinner at 200 yards with a .22, but up close, harumph," Grandma Fred snorted. "He'll be convinced he's plunging the toilet when he's actually fucking your prize winning poodle with a dildo. Funny that way. But everyone loves him."

We began the steep ascent up the precipitous path leading to the Entropy Mansion. Miranda drove over a particularly big bump causing Grandma Fred to bang her head against the roof of the hearse then fall back, silenced. I stared at the Carpathian Castle (which, legend says, had been transferred brick by brick from the ancestral home of Bland Entropy in Transylvania) hanging above us like a dark, dark thing. The hearse shook and jittered as we drove up the path, rocks at the edge crumbling beneath the wheels and plunging hundreds of feet to the sidewalk below.

We pulled up and stopped under a massive stone archway fronting the castle. As we got out of the car, a huge wolf-like creature loped out of the house to greet Igor. This beast was about four feet high at the shoulder with longer forelegs than rear and was covered in coarse brown hair from its short, thick tail to its snarling lips. The creature paused to howl at the sky, its lips pulled back revealing razor sharp fangs.

Reminded me of my ex-wife.

"This is my werewolf," Igor introduced, "Vas Ectomorph."

The wolf beast licked Igor's groin with a foot-long, slavering, prehensile tongue. I could see why they were such good friends. Miranda opened the back of the hearse to let Grandma Fred out, but Grandma Fred didn't move.

"Grandma Fred?" inquired Miranda.

When she got no response, Miranda picked up a shillelagh conveniently leaning against the side of the castle and began striking Grandma Fred in the head with it.

"I think you can cut that out," I told her as I grabbed the Celtic club from her hand. "Can't you see she's dead?"

"No, I'm okay," said Grandma Fred, suddenly moving and struggling to get out of the back of the hearse. "I was just napping."

Blood was streaming down Grandma Fred's forehead as Miranda gave her a hand. Just as Grandma Fred stepped out of the rear door, she lost her balance, arms waving at the sky, and fell over the edge of the road. We stood and watched her tumble and bounce her way to the bottom.

It was a long wait.

"Oops," Igor finally said. "She wasn't just our grandmother. She was also the maid."

"Bummer," I sympathized.

"It's okay, really," said Miranda crossing her arms over her chest. "She belonged to a religious sect that considers it a holy act to be pelted with rocks. In fact, the more painful the better. She'll be stuffed and worshipped as a saint by her fellow cult members. It was merely a fortuitous accident, really."

"Why don't you kids run along inside," I instructed. "I'll follow in a few minutes. Igor, I'm going to have to question your werewolf."

"Go right ahead." They skipped inside, holding hands.

I turned to the 500 pound, hairy dog-man and asked, "How long have you known Bland Entropy?"

He responded with a series of howls and grunts that, after two painstaking hours of notation and analysis, I translated as "Ten years. He raised me from a wolf-babe."

"What can you tell me about Bland?"

Our conversation continued haltingly as I translated.

Drool, drool, howl, snarl, growl = "He definitely had a gland problem."

"How do you know?" I pursued.

Snort, drool, howl = "The writing was on the wall." Vas gestured with his paw at the side of the castle where someone had spray painted:

Bland Entropy has a hyper thalamus

"What's the deal with glands?" I asked.

Vas snarled and shook his snout side to side then pawed at the sky.

Woof, woof, woof, snort = "Look. A lymph gland sitting low and voluminous on its nimbus of light. A cumulogland set adrift amongst cantankerous coffee grounds, dripping feral implants, dropping large breasted hints of a better way, a better life."

The guy's a glandulo-fanatic, I thought to myself. I wasn't about to let this clown in on my thoughts.

Snort, snarl, snort = "I'm part of an ever-growing movement that recognizes the centrality of glands. I can only stare in awe, my jaw dropped just above my thyroid gland, at the more experienced glandulophites as they raise glandiosity to unheard of levels. They raise the gland, really, on what it means to love your glands."

Arrooo, arrooo, snarl, ruff, ruff = "I've heard the speakings of leading glandosophers, breaking the unspoken taboo (or perhaps 'barrier' is a better word), to declare the Gland-head and prove it through a set of Cartesian coordinates. Ah, the savage nature of life."

I deduced from the way he emphasized his penultimate ruff, that, if he had been able to speak English, Vas would have pronounced "savage" with a soft "g".

At the conclusion of his speech, Vas broke out a one hitter (apparently already packed), lit up, and took a deep puff. He gestured again, expansively, and spoke while holding in a toke. Cough, cough, cough = "Look down at the town of Nicetown."

So I did.

Snarl, snarl, cough, cough, snort, chicken, choke = "See that forest? Well, those three trees, anyway. The rest of them got cut down to make way for a strip mall. We still call that our forest. Many, many times I have stepped lightly amongst and between the softly sumptuous trees in the forest as I sought to drink from the Holy Gland of glandness."

Oooo, howl, snort, drool, bow wow, slather = "Oh," then Vas howled piercingly, marijuana smoke billowing from his nostrils like Smaug in The Hobbit, "Ye of little faith. Bow down, bow-wow to the fateful finger of the Gland-head!"

Vas. Glandular, unbidden, smoking Kentucky blue grass, screaming about glands. What a tempest in a teapot.

"Shut the fuck up," I snarled, hitting him in the snout a couple times with a rolled up newspaper I conveniently found in my pocket. Aw shit, ruined my only piece of evidence so far. Vas curled up in fear and yelped like a kicked puppy. "I know all about glands, you Rube. Now tell me what you remember about the day Entropy disappeared, or I'll kick the fucking crap out of you."

Whine, whine, snivel, snivel = "It was a pretty nice day. I remember the maid brought me a treat from Gland Mart – a Gland-O-Burger made from cadaver glands and pus."

"Uh huh. Who was in the house that day?"

Rowr, ruff, rowr = "The maid, the butler, Igor and Miranda and me. And probably Custard Nipplewait, Bland's assistant, but I hardly ever saw her. She pretty much lived in Bland's laboratory."

"Anything else?"

Drool, huff, puff = "I heard a big truck pull up to the laboratory door in the back of the house."

"Really?"

Woof, woof = "Absolutely. I was curious so I circled around back. It was a huge moving truck. I didn't see Bland Entropy anywhere, but some very pale skinned guys were carrying beakers, books, shelving, Bunsen burners, chemical vats, brain probes and other devices out of the lab into the truck. Bland's assistant Custard Nipplewait was directing them. I didn't think much of it, but, when they noticed me looking at them, they all jumped into the truck and took off in a real hurry."

Hmmh, this might be a clue. "Did you happen to notice the name of the moving company?"

Rooby, rack = "As a matter of fact, I did notice that it said 'Mad Scientist Moving Company' on the side of the truck."

This suggests one possibility. Perhaps Bland Entropy was kidnapped by a moving company. "Do you remember anything else about that day?"

Roe, ray = "Not particularly. I ate a few neighborhood kids and shit all over the house. That's about it. Now if you'll excuse me, I have a figure drawing class to attend, and I need to head to the store to buy some charcoal, charcoal paper, string, chewing gum, a baseball bat, a vowel, new kidneys and a freeze ray gun."

"All right. Get the fuck outta here."

Vas scampered off, his tail between his legs.

I looked up at the tremendous castle. It was a fascinating mix of Gothic, Baroque and Bauhaus styles. Such eclecticism bespoke tremendous wealth. The kind of wealth that shops at stores which only open by appointment. The kind of wealth that laughs at the gross domestic product of Canada until milk comes out of its nose. The kind of wealth that buys two of everything – even one-of-a-kind items.

The front door was an eight foot tall, four foot wide, two foot deep carved block of Osmium (the densest substance on earth). It's rumored that Jesse Helm's brain is made of this substance. Coincidentally, I get my shoes made from the same material. They last a lifetime that way. The door was very ornate with gold filigree and carved faces of numerous saints known only to the most studious hagiographer. Fortunately, I study saints in my spare time so I was able to recognize Saint John and Saint Christopher as well as several lesser-known saints. There was Saint Jujube, saint of movie candy. He was raised to sainthood for severely flagellating himself to death with a Twizzler®. There was Saint Dantanna, icon to has-been TV detective actors; Saint Bandanna, saint of Frisbee® catching dogs; and Saint

Foffanabanananana, saint to guys who use every line in the book. Lines like "I've never met anyone like you;" and "Most women fall in love with me in three dates, but I can tell you're not like that;" and "With stock options, I earn somewhere between four and five million;" and "I'm sorry, what did you say? I was mesmerized by your face;" and "I've never had such scintillating conversation;" and "If you touch the Poisonous Arrow Frog, identifiable by its bright yellow bands, your muscles will contract violently until you enter a state similar to rigor mortis; then, while you are still conscious, bugs will eat your eyes." That last one has never failed to get me laid.

I pushed open the perfectly balanced front door with my index finger and entered the mansion. To my left was a large planter containing a topiary tree trimmed into an exact likeness of Chrissy, Janet and Jack from *Three's Company*. To my right was a four foot high model of a scrotum. It may have been the largest scrotum I'd ever seen - very detailed with wrinkles, delicate hairs and weighty testicles. All I could think was, "Très élégante."

A seven and a half foot tall African-American man in a stylish Armani tuxedo came toward me, holding out his hand.

"Welcome, welcome. You must be Satan Donut." He shook my hand politely. "My Vagina told me to expect you. I'm their butler, Manute Bol. I see you're looking at the scrotum. You might be interested to learn that that is the Entropy family crest."

"Interesting," I said. "I thought family crests were found on shields and such."

"Well, in the case of the Entropy family, the men were particularly regarded for their cock fighting. Bland traces his line all the way back to David of Israel. According to the Entropy family legend, David did not slay the giant with a sling but by fwapping him with his large balls."

"Now-a-days that might be considered a friendly gesture," I noted. "Say, I thought you played basketball in the NBA."

"I did," he explained, "but a terrible accident took me out of the game permanently."

"What happened?" I asked.

As he spoke, Manute touched his eyebrow pensively, as if to say, *Here's my eyebrow.* "I was in the hospital for a routine boil lancing when they mixed me up with another patient who had an incapacitating fear of heights. They surgically removed my vertical leap. Even worse, they neglected my boil which got so bad my entire posterior fell off. I was in line for a transplant, but no butts were about at the time. I put out a booty call, but no one answered."

He shrugged his shoulders with resignation. "I was cut from the NBA for poor performance so I took a stint as a ventriloquist. I would go to the local five and dime (or Seven-Eleven as they call it these days due to inflation) and perform using my large intestine as a hand puppet. I modeled my style after the great Edgar Bergen but was also influenced by Frank Gorshin as well as, of course, Caligula who was well known for his puppeteering. Sometimes with proper lighting, my intestines looked like Mother Theresa."

The great Bol went on, "I decided that I needed to get serious so I applied to college and was accepted at Harvard to study Molecular Biology. I was offered a work study job as a butler for Bland Entropy which was very exciting because Bland is one of the world's most renowned molecular biologists."

"What was your relationship with Bland like?"

"Unfortunately, not as rewarding as I had hoped." Manute shook his head in obvious disappointment. "He's a very secretive man. He dyed his hair weekly, wore colored contacts, and used a voice modulator. He also used stilts and body padding to disguise his height and weight. He never looked the same from day to day. Once, I let a pygmy chieftain have the run of the house for an entire day before I realized it wasn't Dr. Entropy. I began sneaking into Bland's private laboratory at night just to figure out what the hell he was working on."

Manute turned his eyes toward the ceiling as he thoughtfully reminisced with me about Bland. "Despite all that, golly do I miss him. I miss the pungent smell of his sweat. I miss the beads of dew that collected in his eyebrows. The dandruff spread like fresh snow on his shoulders. I miss the twitch in his left eye when he was being coy. I miss the great width of his calves as they filled his silken stockings clipped to his lingerie with care."

"What kind of research was he doing?" I pursued.

Manute led me out of the hallway into the kitchen area as he continued speaking, "I discovered he focused on two disciplines. One was meteorology. He had computer graphs and tables of temperature measurements from around the world. He had particulate counters, smog readers, volumetric carbon dioxide tubes, thermometers, rain slickers, snow boots, leaf blowers, and even an open window through which he could look to evaluate what the weather was like on any given day. It was clear that he wanted to know the weather."

The entire kitchen was made from translucent blue plastic. It was very hip, very now. We had a seat at the kitchen table, and Manute brought us some Decaf iced mocha latté espressos before he proceeded. "His second area of interest was insects. He had hundreds of insects both live and dissected. Grasshoppers, stag beetles, cockroaches, ants, butterflies, walking sticks, spiders, and politicians. He had electron microscopes with which he was examining the DNA of various insects as well as devices to bombard them with radiation. He had small ovens, freezers and gas chambers. He seemed to be evaluating different ways to kill insects.

"There was even some evidence that insects were killing themselves rather than undergoing Bland's fiendish experiments. I found a ladybug hanging by a thread."

"What else did his lab contain?" I asked.

"He had an extensive library of scientific texts on genetics and biology both animal and human. There was usually an array of cadavers and tools for dissection. Sometimes, when he had too many cadavers in rigor mortis, I would find them all over the place. I've seen them used as coffee tables, coat racks, hanging mobiles, a see-saw, a cat scratching post, a stairmaster, an ant farm, a fourth in Bridge, and also a golf bag. Other items in his laboratory included Bunsen burners, a huge variety of chemicals, mini-nuclear reactors, left-over donuts, laser surgery tools, and a collection of mother-of-pearl cock rings."

"This espresso is really good, I gotta tell you. What can you tell me about the day Bland disappeared?" I inquired.

"As usual, I served him his breakfast promptly at 8:15am. The same food he always eats: an egg sandwich, half an overripe banana, a Whitman's Sampler, and a Bomb Pop. He read *USA Today* with breakfast but only for the advertise-ments. Usually, he's very taciturn, but once I heard him chortle to himself and mutter, 'That Marmaduke.'

"On the particular day in question, out of nowhere, he turned and spoke to me. 'What do you know about the end of the world?' he asked me.

"I thought for a moment then told him, 'I think it would hurt.'

"'You wanna know about physical pain?' he challenged me. 'Imagine having to piss really, really bad, and your bladder is filling to burst, but there's nowhere to go, and you have to keep holding and holding. You're about to explode, and your penis is crushed up against your jeans like a wet salami with elephantiasis.' He paused and then mumbled to himself, 'I think I need breakaway clothes,' before addressing me again, 'Did you ever see that movie Full Velcro Jacket? Never mind. That's what the end of the world will feel like.'"

At this point, Manute started getting a little choked up.

"Buck up, tin soldier," I consoled him with a hand on the shoulder. "Have some more espresso."

He finally pulled himself together after gulping down an oversized demitasse. "Bland got up from the table and went outside to putter around in the garden. He loved...loves his marigolds. I was a little concerned about him because I heard reports on the news the previous evening about herds of violent mimes ravaging the countryside. The news commentators are calling this the 'War for the Mimes of America.' The mimes are very difficult to catch because they always have the advantage of complete silence. I was concerned that Bland might be attacked, so I went directly to bed and took a nap.

"When I woke up eight hours later, he was gone. I suspect Bland was kidnapped and perhaps eaten by wild mimes."

"That's certainly a possibility," I agreed. "I'll look into it. Thank you for the helpful information you've provided." We shook hands, and, as he walked me to the front door, I queried him one more question, "I've always wanted to ask you about your name. It's rather ironic, don't you think?"

"Yes. It's the greatest irony of my life. I don't even like bowling." With that, he walked off.

CHAPTER 4

To: Ratat@calm.com (Satan Donut)
From: Joydivision@dot.com (Etta Donut)
Subject: Weeping Anal Polyps

Practice is through and, as usual, it was fucked up.
Spitto came in drunk off his ass and puked all over his
snare drum. Why is it so hard to find a drummer who
isn't a disaster case? But at least, after he puked, his
head was clear enough to play. I kind of like the way
it sounds with the drum a beat behind.

By the way, I started fucking our lead guitarist because
I was bored. It's probably not a great idea, but I never
trusted "great ideas" anyway. They're usually thought up

by "great men." Rodent is a genius guitarist. That's the only good thing I can say about him really. Otherwise he's a huge, arrogant prick.

This is my current favorite song we're doing called Pursuit of Happiness:

Heavy head leaning,
Lying while sitting,
Bone white mind.
A toad sitting on the tarmac and a car rushing
Rushing up my esophagus
Catching in my throat.
Halfway thru existentialism I'm caught
At the point where you invent the meaning.
Whip snarl cold in the dead of winter
A vacant lot,
Strips of peeling paint mark spaces,
Cracks in the firmament,
And a hurtling apocalypse.
Vaguely, I'm aware that I spill
Poison from my lips and thighs.
I'm wandering across broken bottles,
bricks, unreadable signs, gasoline fumes, grim mutterings,
to face a blank stare at home.
—Fuckface

To: Joydivision@dot.com (Etta Donut)
From: Ratat@calm.com (Satan Donut)
Subject: Sigmund Floyd the Barber

You're last email was most interesting. But, no, I'm afraid I can't help you with that phobia of pants you've developed. On the other hand, thanks for your advice about my "concerns." I had never thought to use a Weed Whacker in the manner you suggested.

Yesterday, I was busy invading Canada. Canada didn't seem to mind so maybe we'll have a second date.

I appreciate your provocative insights into the mating rituals of the Australian Beaver. I've also been very impressed with your song writing abilities. You have inspired me to dig deep and write my own poem. It's called Forest and it goes a-something like this:

I play checkers with an ancient wren.
He opens a strategic can of whup ass to defeat me.
However, I wrestle him into submission.
Never beat a human at checkers. If you're a wren, any-way. Never mind that. This is a poem not a tip sheet for fucking birds.
Death is a tangy sauce. Yum.
—Christopher Marlowlife

Sponsored by Westinghouse-GE-Disney®.
We define reality. Thank you very much.™

CHAPTER

I decided to follow up on the hot lead I got from Manute Bol.
I went out the front door and performed a thorough search
of the garden. I found the marigolds had been trampled flat.
There were many shoe prints in the garden that left no
tread marks - just flat indentations. The slipper marks of
roving mimes?

I circled around the back of the mansion. There was a large
door with a handle at the bottom. It appeared similar in
many ways to the kind of door you might refer to as a "garage
door," but I didn't want to jump to any conclusions. It's
important to eliminate all preconceived notions when
putting clues together to solve a mystery or puzzle. Unless
it's the kind of puzzle whose parts are preconceived
notions. A cement road led away from this "door" and
around the house in the opposite direction. I tugged the door
upward to reveal a large room. The floor was bare cement,

uncarpeted. It did not look comfortable. There was a mini-hearse parked on one side of the room and a Ferrari Testerosa on the other. There was hardly room for a settee.

There was a line in the opposite wall. The line formed a rectangle with the shorter part at the top and bottom and the longer part on the right and left. There was a doorknob on the right hand edge of this line but within its confines. It appeared to be similar to what you might describe as a "regular door." I surmised that one might turn the doorknob and enter another room. I opened this so-called "regular door" to reveal a very narrow room with two doors on the right and one at the far end. To the naive eye, this room might be referred to as a "hallway." But I knew it was more, oh so much more. It was the locus of all that was good and evil in the world. Or maybe it was just a hallway.

The first door to the right had a sign above it reading:

The second door had a sign above it reading:

The third door had a sign above it reading:

An amateur sleuth might feel the need to put on a pirate costume and dance wildly until exhausted, flop to the ground, and pick a door based on the final direction of his flopping. However, with my expansive experience in these matters, I knew that it was better to pull out my chicken bones and toss them on the ground. I did so and then interpreted the pattern formed by the bones with a complex and arcane symbology much like that found in deconstructionist critical theory. This interpretation led me to the door marked "Bathroom." This made excellent sense since I had to piss really badly.

I opened the door. It was a small room with a toilet, sink, and a mirror above the sink. I peed in the sink then stole the roll of toilet paper off its roller. Boy, I remember in the 80's when that huge debate raged in Ann Landers about whether the roll should hang with the free end closer to the wall or away from the wall. Now I can look back on it and laugh, but, at the time, it was the most traumatic event in my childhood.

I yanked on the toilet paper roller, and it moved smoothly outward like a safe deposit box, still attached to the two steel posts on either end. I twisted it counter-counter-clockwise, and the wall behind the toilet swung outward.

Let's just say I had a hunch. (And the chicken bones have never led me astray.) (Except that time I took the fork in the river which led me down a hundred foot waterfall.)

(Although, I wouldn't call that astray so much as really, really, painfully wrong.)

I went through the opening in the wall and entered a large room with a high ceiling. A phone rang. There was a phone sitting on a coffee table by the entryway. I picked up the phone.

"Hello?"

"Satan, it's your mother," said my mother.

"I know that."

"Listen. We had the most awful experience I need to tell you about."

"Mom, I'm investigating right now."

"What? You're too busy for your mother? Let me get your dad on the line, this'll only take a minute...Dad! Hey Papa!"

Off in the distance I hear, "I'm coming. I'm coming." Then another line picked up. "Hokay, it's Papa. Now what'r you tryin' to do, give me a heart attack?"

"Oh, you," said Mom, "Listen. We need to warn you. There's a restaurant here, the Black Orchid."

"American cuisine," interrupted Dad.

"And we went in there to eat, and there was almost no one there."

"We asked why and the waitress said, 'Oh, it's just that time of day,'" explained Dad.

"So you got a what? A roast beef," Mom stated.

"Steak," Dad corrected her.

"And I got a steak. Dad ordered his well done and mine medium well. When the steaks came, they were both pink."

"Raw."

"Raw. So Dad said, 'Excuse me. I ordered well done,' and the waitress said, 'Oh. I'm sorry,' and took it back. Well, we had to send it back three times. And also, when we ordered dinner we ordered the French Onion soup. The menu said dinner includes soup, but when we got the bill we were charged extra for the soup. We said, 'Excuse me, but isn't the soup included?' And she said, 'Not the French Onion,' and we said, 'Well, shouldn't you have told us that?' When we went up to the woman to pay with our credit card, the woman asked us if everything was fine and we said, 'No, Dad's steak was raw and had to be sent back three times, and we were charged for soup even though it said soup included.' And it was like, Whoosh! Nothing. Like we hadn't even spoken. Like we were on another planet. Not even a 'Sorry.'"

"When did this happen, Mom?" I asked.

"About six months ago."

"Okay, I won't go to the Black Orchid Restaurant. Now I gotta go. Bye." And I hung up.

I looked around the room. There was a mess of papers in boxes, but all the machines had been removed. I went through the stacks of papers. Among the debris, I found maps tracking storms, tornadoes, hurricanes, monsoons, and tsunamis. There were reams of data from weather satellites and truck weighing stations around the world. I was about to give up when I noticed – jammed between a report on the boiling point of maggots and a copy of some nudie magazine featuring the girls of Gamma Alpha Yeti in Catholic school girl outfits – a couple of handwritten receipts. Bland had made several payments of $10,000 to one "A. Mime." Abe Mime? Aaron Mime?

I spotted some white streaks on the wall that made me curious. They were the same color as the white marks on the brick heaved through the window of my office. I took a sample and dipped it into my Mini-Chemalyzer. The results were clear: Ferrigno's Pancake Make-Up, the kind most commonly used by mimes.

I put it all together: Looks like the mimes were blackmailing Bland and finally decided to kidnap him for some nefarious purpose. And they had sent me a brick telegram to warn me off the case. I had to find those mimes.

I heard a noise behind me. Whirled around, drawing my AK-47. A woman was standing by the secret entrance. She had stringy, mousy hair, a lumpy, pear shaped body with a flat chest, a short, flat nose, and thick glasses that made her gray eyes appear twice their normal size. She blinked like an owl then turned and ran. This must be Bland's assistant, Custard Nipplewait, returning to get the remaining papers. I suspected she was in with the mimes.

I made after her. She was low to the ground and fast; by the time I got outside, she was already hopping into a car. I performed a diving forward roll just as she turned the ignition. I latched onto the rear bumper and hung on as she squealed away. We swung around the house and bumped down the precipitous path, but I clung to the bumper tenaciously.

When we hit the street below, she began weaving side to side, evidently trying to shake me off. But they don't call me "The Sucker" for nothing. She drove down a cobblestone road and over a series of speed bumps, yet I stuck like an octopus. Then she went over a pile of broken glass, across a field of hot coals, into the Schick razor blade factory, and through a Cambodian land mine field. Finally she pulled over at a Piggly Wiggly. She must've thought she'd lost me because she got out and walked down the sidewalk at a determined pace but without running. I waited a few moments and then followed her at a discrete distance.

She entered a Walgreens twenty yards ahead. It was time to close in for the kill. I donned a bright red wig, a matching nose, and large red flippers before slipping into the Walgreens. I made my way slowly down the makeup aisle, lingering by the blush just long enough to perform a brief touch up on the cheeks. Custard wasn't in sight, so I moved on to the pharmaceutical department then looked carefully up each aisle - no sign of her!

The Walgreens was oddly silent. It was unusual that no one was in the store. Then I noticed a suspicious bulge in a Smokeless Ashtray refill box.

It was her. My god! – I'd been made! Caught flat footed, looking like a Bozo.

I dove into the fake-foam sponge bin and held my breath. I doffed the wig and nose, obviously a failure. I decided I would have to disguise myself with something more subtle to fool this dame. I would imitate a Hallmark Greeting Card. She'd never expect that. But dammit, which one? I struck myself repeatedly in the forehead with a fake-foam sponge trying to trigger an idea. Then it came to me: a congratulatory card I had sent to my cousin Charlene Nobyl who had had a baby recently. The card read on the outside:

Having a three legged, four armed, toothless, asexual baby?

The inside of the card contained the following poem:

What great news that your kid won't need braces,
And it'll win all the Three-Legged races.
You'll get twice as many hugs as most parents, with ease,
And never have to worry about it getting a sexual disease.
If you didn't live downstream from that factory pollutant,
You would never have had such a cuddly little mutant!

I made my way toward the counter disguised as the Hallmark congratulatory card, and there she was by the cash register posing as a rope of Beef Jerky. I gotta say, nice skintight plastic wrapper. I was about to whip out my credit card to purchase that little filet when she gave me the slip. It was a very nice slip, too - gold, shimmery but not too gaudy. I was distracted. Color, shiny color, and my size, too. By the time I looked up, she was gone.

What a disaster! Foiled again. This woman was good. Damn good.

Just then I realized I had to rush home, or I was going to miss some seriously good TV. There were a lot of good commercials on television tonight, and I didn't want to miss them. I always go through my Television Guide (the most read magazine in the world) and highlight all the commercials and shows I particularly want to watch. I took a bus back to the bowling alley and rode my hog home. I live in a hermetically sealed plastic dome at the top of Tom & Dick Hill.

Sometimes I wish I was someone else.

When I got home, I headed straight for the Lay-Z-Boy and flicked on the TV with a verbal command. It was a made-for-TV movie entitled "Love In the Third Degree Burn Ward." The scene - a beach at dusk with a lone figure looking out over the ocean. A man's voice-over came in narrating the story. The guy sounded like he'd just inhaled a deck of cigs and forgot to exhale the smoke.

"A putrid tide washes ashore. Bits of bone, rat carcasses, cigarette butts, oil slicks, foaming chemicals, and the body of Simon Lazar. He was a slimy underworld Kingpin, and I was the cop assigned to the case."

A second guy entered the scene and walked up next to the first guy. This second guy, stilting up on stick figure legs, had a rail thin waist and huge shoulders making him looking like a giant mushroom. This second guy was dragging the body of a third guy on a rope behind him. The first guy spoke, revealing himself to be the narrator. "What have you got for me, Deltoid?"

The second guy, named Deltoid, bent down and looked at the third guy. "He appears to have been forced to the surface and has been floating for several days. From the frayed rope on his leg, it would appear he was given the old Deep Six treatment. And perhaps a hot cream rinse, as well."

"Nails?" asked the first figure.

"He had a pedicure just before death," replied Deltoid while examining the body's feet.

"Aha!" said the first figure.

"What does that tell you, Spank?" asked Deltoid.

Then the voice-over returned, "That's me. Spank Pancreas, Police Detective - twice removed."

"Nothing. It just reminds me that I need to get my nails done," explained Spank.

I liked this Spank Pancreas, first guy, leader of other guys of various numbers.

"I'll begin questioning suspects immediately," declared Spank, never taking his eyes off the ocean.

Spank Pancreas stripped naked and performed a graceful pirouette followed by an entrechat and a fiddle-dee-dee. He walked to a dinghy nearby, pulled a wetsuit out of the boat, and began putting it on over his oh-so naked form. He put on a facemask, flippers and an air tank. Then he swam into the water and descended below the water line. As he did, the voice-over returned, "I waded into the ocean and sank beneath the surface. I was going to crack this case no matter what it took."

Spank came face to face with an off blue Parrot Fish. He grabbed the fish by the fins and slammed him against a rock. "Okay, Parrot. Start bubbling."

"I don't know nuthin'" dummied up the Parrot fish.

Spank hooked a finger deeper into his gills. "We're talking about a body thrown to the surface a couple days ago."

All right, I'd seen enough of this program. It was plainly obvious that the President's albino twin, a collection of pantaloons, and some machine gun toting Canadian Geese were not only responsible for killing Simon Lazar (who was trying to muscle in on their profitable sale of consciousness) but they were also busy selling the Laws of Physics to the highest bidder resulting in having to pay Westinghouse-GE-Disney® for the right to have gravity in your house. Yeah, yeah. I could see it coming from a mile away. Can't anyone write an original script any more?

I switched channels to another show about thirty-year-olds with expensive haircuts pretending to be clever twenty-year-olds. This was one of my least favorite shows, but since it was so popular it had some of the coolest commercials.

My Lay-Z-Boy put a sucker on my penis and jerked me off as I excitedly waited for the commercials. As I was building toward my peak of orgasm, two especially memorable ads played.

The first opened with an half-naked woman (sometimes she's missing the left side of her outfit, other times the right) asleep on a bus. The voice over said, "Narcolepsy! That's right, you too can have your very own special case of Narcolepsy for only $199.99 plus $2000 shipping and handling. Never will sleepless nights haunt you again. Never will you be tired. Why? Because you'll be asleep most of the time! You won't even notice."

They cut to the woman asleep at her desk in the office, then asleep propped in a chair during an obviously important business meeting. You could tell it's important because there were many flowcharts and graphs displayed and a stern looking man wearing suspenders who had the word ASSHOLE tattooed on his forehead. "Boring meetings? Sleep through them," said the voice-over.

Then they cut to the woman curled up on the kitchen counter while a husband figure yells at her. "Relationship problems? Sleep on it."

Next the woman was dangling by ropes from the ceiling while being penetrated from behind by a flabby, sweaty gentleman with hair on his back. "Sex problems? Sleep around!"

Finally, they showed the woman asleep on a street corner with a bottle of Jack Daniel's in her hand. "Alcoholic? Sleep it off. And, if you order now, you'll get a free case of Botulism! So send in your checks immediately to Dr. Plasterpenis, 6969 South End, Bottoms Up, SC 02134."

The second ad consisted of a locked down shot of a naked woman with breasts so large they obscured most of her torso. It appeared as though two skin colored watermelons had been glued to her ribcage. The breasts were supported by two Doric pedestals.

She spoke, "Hello. I'm a copywriter at Leo Burnett. They asked me to write an ad for Coors Beer. I said, 'I don't think so.' You see, I don't write ads. They write themselves. Occasionally, they come to me in a dream. Either that, or they don't get written at all. So, instead, I'll just talk into this tape recorder..." She holds up a hand-held tape recorder, "...and have my creative assistant transcribe my ideas. I refuse to write. After all, isn't this supposed to be a paperless society? But we all know that's really bullshit. All right, my point is that I will sleep with you if you buy Coors beer. I promise."

I gave a verbal command to my television, and a Coors Beer was delivered to me from the Product-Materializer in the top of the TV set. Finally, I came into my Lay-Z-Boy sucker and drifted off into a comfortable sleep.

To: Ratat@calm.com (Satan Donut)
From: Joydivision@dot.com (Etta Donut)
Subject: Uglife

They have asked me politely not to return to the department I was working for. What is their fucking goddamn
fucking problem? Whinella from my temp agency called me
this morning and said that the bitch I was working for
said I was too NEGATIVE. I'll show her negative. I'll
turn her the fuck inside out. And I'm positive I will.

I convinced Whinella that the bitch at the advertising
agency was the psycho one. After all, she's the one who
made me sharpen her thumbtacks every morning. Even so,

if I get another complaint against me it'll be hard to
get more temp work. Fuck it anyway.

By the way, thanks for the poem. Do I sense a growing
Robert Barrett Browning? A ripe Kenneth Rexroth? A ten-
der Robert Frost? On second thought, the answer is no.
Stick to what you know best, beating heads.

On the lighter side of darkness, things are going well
with Rodent. We enjoyed a bloodletting ritual last night
and summoned the spirit of Beelzebub. To his chagrin and
my joy, he seems to have grown two extra penises (peni?)
because of the ceremony. You can't beat that. Well, you
could, but you'd need an extra hand. Rodent is basical-
ly an asshole, but he gives me great orgasms. I wrote a
song yesterday dedicated to him:

Temporary Anesthesia

Sometimes the world spreads out before me like ground
glass.
If I think about it too much, my mind will shred like
Iran-Contra evidence.
It helps to kick the impossible around, beat it up,
shake it down.
You can't use the word "dream" anymore without it sound-
ing like a fuck-toy of the corporate elite.

I imagine a world without money.

75

I pretend I can live a life of freedom.
I want to squeeze time and drip it on you like honey.

We live in an 18 screen cinema world,
each makes me scream louder than the next.
Ozone depletion,
Car zone completion.
I spew my twisted verbal wreckage on a vampire empire
that coats my rivers with sewage.
And the only river I can swim in is the golden stream
of your hair.

Politics is a waste of time, but if we don't waste our
time they'll waste us faster.
We've called a plenary session of the Knights of
Inevitable Drippage,
The steering committee recommends anal penetration of
the corporate domain with the Scud Missiles of anxiety
that hunt my dreams.

Peace is the temporary anesthesia I inhale when we kiss.
I want a cartoon world without real world payback.
E-Racer X all the politician's lies.
The only blue skies left are in your eyes.

To: Joydivision@dot.com (Etta Donut)
From: Ratat@calm.com (Satan Donut)
Subject: Far from Nugent

I'm not averse in my universe to averring your verse as
very diverse. Is this version, Vern, a diversion from
your unique patina of batique? Or is it, rather, a lath-
er of salve on a baroque joke?

Since you enjoyed my last poem so much I thought I'd put
finger to keyboard and conjure another magical master-
piece inspired by your story. This one is untitled:

Mephifuckingstopheles
Beelzefuckingbub
Terence Trent Darby
The Soul Train dancing club.

Let me know what you think. Been playing my Andy Gibb
solo album over and over as reference material. Sorry
you lost another job.

-Greg Airy, u.s.

I woke up refreshed, but, as I licked my lips, I realized why my mouth felt like rubber cement. I had forgotten to brush my teeth the night before, and they'd fallen out. I picked them off my shirt like lint. The sharp roots of some of my teeth had hooked into the chain-links in my bulletproof vest. Other teeth had dropped into the creases in my pants. I collected them all and went to the bathroom where I put them in the ToothBrite® by Machine-0® where they whirred around for a bit until I put my mouth on the Glue-Tooth Tube® by Machine-0®, and my teeth were jammed back into my gums. (Machine-0®. We make machines because you're so fucked up.™)

I put the TV back on while eating a bowl of Sparkling Puke

Bits® from Quaker Oats®. I flipped to ESPN 4 and was pleased to see they were rebroadcasting this year's Annual Spit-Take Contest from Innsbruck. Marv Albert, the host, announced the rules.

"The rules are simple. Contestants come up to the Spit Line." They showed a close-up of a thick red line, followed by a slow dolly back.

"And then our straight man," camera cuts to Buddy Hackett, "delivers the cue line, 'Uncle Tannous is coming to town,'" Buddy Hackett waved half-heartedly, "and then the competitors let loose for all they're worth! They will be judged on Distance, Diffusion, Timing and Evening Gown."

Cut to panel of judges: Leo DiCaprio and the Spice Girls (who are in their 40s these days and out of shape but still spunky).

Cut to Buddy giving the cue line followed by a Yugoslavian competitor spit-taking. This was followed in quick succession by the famous Bruni Arpeggio from Italy and Rondelle Bondo from Venezuela. Music by the Dave Matthews Band played as the editing sped up, showing competitor after competitor spit-taking from a variety of angles. This sequence was intercut with shots of the judges holding up scores or occasionally throwing their ranking cards on the ground, sleeping on top of the judge's table and even holding up their middle fingers in lieu of a numbered card.

Finally we returned to Marv Albert, "And the results? Taking the Spit-Take world by storm is newcomer Ted Bleg." Ted appeared in a lovely evening gown and tiara, interspersed with slow-motion shots of the winningest spit-take.

I switched the channel over to The Update Channel [The Update Channel. We Take Crappy Old Shit and Make It New.™] They were showing an adaptation of Les Miserables called "Les' Miserable Clothes." The main character was this guy named Les who was scarred as a child because he had a bad haircut at the Jean Valjean Salon. He grew up to hate all well groomed men. Yet, he was convinced that with just the right outfit he could become one of the "in crowd." He pursued the elusive "perfect fit" for over 40 years, but eventually committed suicide when he realized he'd put on so much weight eating French soufflés he could no longer fit into his tweed bouclé jacket and Versace tights. The ending of the adapted-for-cable movie was very touching. I cried as they showed a dramatic close-up of the suicide knife penetrating through Les' cotton shirt from The Gap. [The Gap. When you want to be like everyone else.™] It's sad to see a perfectly good shirt like that ruined.

My eyes were puffy and red, and my vision clouded from crying, as I made my way to take a shower. I was walking naked from my kitchen to the bathroom when I accidentally tripped and fell on two giant grizzly bear traps I leave set to catch intruders. One sprung on the loose flesh below my armpit. The other snapped onto my left testicle causing me to gasp loudly and fall backwards. As I gasped, two hornets and a scorpion I keep as pets were sucked into my larynx, and I was stung repeatedly in my mouth and esophagus. My backward momentum caused me to fall directly into my cactus terrarium. While climbing from the ten foot deep cactus pit I use as a terrarium, I knocked over my 55 gallon drum of rubbing alcohol which soaked into every prick left by the cacti in my skin and some went in my eyes. I swelled up to twice my normal size.

This situation might put a damper on sleuthing for a lesser investigator, but I knew that a little logical thinking should fix things up in a jiffy. Since I had nearly doubled my weight in pus, I decided the best thing to do was to go to the gym and work it off. But there was no time to actually go to the gym so I just imagined going instead.

When I walked into the gym in my imagination, it was very humdrum. The piped in music was violin solos by Brahms or some such shit. A few people were working out, but there was no energy. Everyone looked bored. I overheard the manager saying to the spinning coach, "This is horrible. This place has become dull, dull, dull. And on a Friday night! We have to do something."

"Let me make a call," I said to him.

I grabbed a phonebook, found the entertainment section, and turned to a listing that said, "The Fun Bunch." I gave them a call. Someone enthusiastically picked up, "Fun Bunch!"

I pleaded with the man, "Can you help us Fun Bunch? Our gym has become dull, dull, dull."

"No problem," he responded. "We'll be right over."

No sooner had I hung up the phone than the gym door burst open revealing three men dressed in feather boas, platform shoes, huge neon rimmed sunglasses and Spandex. One guy was on roller skates. As they swept in, the music changed to "Stayin' Alive," and balloons and streamers dropped from the ceiling.

The big jock using the hack squat looked at them with distaste, but, when one of the Fun Guys popped over and stroked the big guy's leg, he was won over and began squatting excitedly. Another fun guy leapt onto the stairmaster where a woman was struggling. He began singing "I Will Survive" by Gloria Gaynor at the top of his lungs as he marched with her on the stairmaster. Soon she was high stepping with the best of the them. The third Fun Guy took over the aerobics class causing a disco ball to drop from the ceiling, and before you knew it everyone was lying on the ground gasping for air.

The phone jarred me from my reverie. I was pleasantly surprised to discover that I'd managed to work off all my pus.

Then I looked again and realized the pus had drained into my knees which were the size of the revamped VW Beatle. [VW Beatle. Buy one, and you'll have more friends.™] I used a rusty butter knife to slash my knees which drained out the pus. Ah, much better.

I had to figure out what to do next, but it was difficult to get my bearings. When it comes to finding my bearings, I'm usually screwed. Nuts. I was missing a certain...I don't know what.

It came to me that the next step was to answer the phone which had been ringing insistently for several minutes now. The caller ID told me it was Jenny Sayqua. She's my faithful sidekick. We go way back. Back in 1998 we used to do X and go clubbing together. We'd pick up transvestites and roll them for spare change. Not hurt them or anything, we'd just pick them up and roll them like a haircurler – a big haircurler that you could roll on the ground. We'd roll them, and then if any spare change fell out of their purse or fake boobs or whatever, we'd pick it up.

Jenny and I were in WWIII together. Well, not actually. We used to play the computer game. She'd be the corporate controlled countries, and I'd be the rebel capitalist countries. God, we stayed up all night sometimes playing that game.

We were such close friends that she could pick my toe jam, and I'd smooth out her camel toe. And there was no sex involved. At least not on my part. Sometimes she'd stare really hard at me and tell me she had a psychic orgasm. But if I tried to whip it out and jack off, she'd scream bloody murder and shoot rubber bands at my penis which can really hurt if they get you right on the tip. Other than that, she was a great person. Anyway, I better answer the phone.

"Satan, it's Jenny," she said with her raspy baritone.

"You're absolutely correct. Now, listen close, this is urgent. I've got very little time. I'm on this new case. Gotta find this Bland Entropy guy. I need you to do some research on him. Find newspaper articles, books, photos, look stuff up on microfilm, computers, internet. Think of it as an extended music video sequence within a movie."

"I don't think so. I'm calling to get that $100 you owe me from the last time I walked your dog."

That dog. Forgot about him. Hope he's still alive somewhere. "Right, right, how about I pay you after you do the research."

"You never even pay me a fucking salary, jerk."

"Perhaps our friendship is payment enough."

"You little slimeball. I should take my foot and ram it so far up your ass you'll need a crowbar to get it out. I'm gonna remove your torso until you're nothing but a head sitting on top of two legs. Twist you up like a linguini flapping in the wind," Jenny screamed.

"That's the spirit. So when can I expect the information?"

"How about the 5th of Never?"

"Sounds good. I'll be waiting."

"Why don't you take a slow boat to Switzerland."

"An excellent suggestion. Get back to me with more information later. I've got a boat to catch."

I called up my travel agent and booked a slow boat to Zurich. Conveniently, Princess Cruise Lines has a ship leaving every hour. I rode to the dock and caught the boat.

Two weeks later I was in Zurich. I rented a land speeder and skimmed to where Interlaken used to be. Interlaken was formerly a tourist area, but now the Alps are used as a giant garbage can – all the valleys filled up almost to the snow line. I dropped off the speeder and took a tram to the small village of Gimmelwald. I checked in at the Xerox-Cannon® Bed & Breakfast and promptly took a nap. When I woke up, refreshed, I went and sat on the creaky old wood balcony drinking a Milwaukee's Best® and staring at the tiny peaks poking out of the piles of putrid, rotting garbage. It doesn't get any better than this.

I stayed drunk for three days, but Bland Entropy never showed up. I was thinking that Jenny's tip was no good when, out of the blue, a very suspicious event occurred. On the third morning, I was sipping my first Bloody Mary of the day on the rickety old porch of my B & B when I heard the familiar sound of a grav copter nearby. Actually, grav copters are silent, but that silent sound is very familiar to me from the many times I'd spent asleep hearing silence. So this grav copter comes around a pile of garbage into sight, and there's this horned cow (a bull, I guess) in a harness dangling as peaceful as could be looking at the ground below him. It must've been really fascinating for that cow. I mean, cows can't jump so this must have been the first time he'd ever seen the ground at any distance further from his head than the height of his head above the ground. I wish I could be that easily defamiliarized from my surroundings. I squinted at the cow as it floated by and realized that there was something dangling between his legs. It was the Entropy family crest! So I hopped off the porch and ran after the cow. Fortunately, the grav copter didn't go too far; it dropped the cow off at a farm just down the path.

I slowed down to catch my breath and walked up to the front porch of the farmhouse. A distinguished middle-aged man in overalls was seated on a rocking chair with his legs up on the railing. His head was back as he stroked his beard and stared at the grey sky. I approached him and asked if he parlez vous Anglais.

"Sure, can I help you?"

"That cow that just got cowlifted here. I saw it. I recognized its balls."

The farmer stopped stroking his beard to consider me thoughtfully. He paused for a minute before replying. "I suppose you might've."

There, he'd admitted it. This farm must be owned by Bland Entropy. I knew there was a connection. "Tell me," I pursued. "What do you know about Entropy?"

He began biting his lip, acting a bit edgy, looking around. He probably wanted to make sure no one was spying on us. "I know that Entropy will be the ruin of everything."

"I knew it! I knew Entropy had some dastardly plan. Where can I find this Entropy?"

"If I tell you, will you please go away and never come back?" asked the farmer. Obviously he was concerned that Entropy might kill him if he tipped me off.

"Of course. Your secret is safe with me," I reassured him.

"Okay. Look where things decay. Now I gotta go hide in my closet, okay?"

"Great. Thanks for the info."

A clue! This was great news. I pondered what he had told me as I went back to the bed and breakfast to collect my baggage and check out. I immediately caught a quick slow boat back to Los Angeles.

As soon as I reached LA, I got on my hog and rode. Rode like the wind. I wanted to be free. Free from the man. There's nothing like riding a big hog at sixty miles per hour, the wind in your face, the hog bristles jabbing your thighs. I do my best thinking while riding Rush. I rode so fast that my lips blew off. I had to circle back and pick them up, and, as I bent down to pick them up, it dawned on me what the farmer meant by "Look where things decay." It was time for a Zombie hunt.

Zombies are fun because they're, like, already dead.

So I rode my hog to Pariah Town to fuck up some Zombies and see what they could tell me about Bland Entropy's location. Generally, the best way to interrogate a Zombie is to bitch slap them. You can paste their damned faces against a wall. You can remove their limbs. Whatever. I admit, it's a lot of fun. Also, I enjoy beating them with Bibles. There's nothing like a good Zombie Bible beating. Lepers are fun, too, but not as much fun as Zombies because Lepers aren't dead yet. Sometimes Lepers become Zombies, and that's good. I think Adobe makes a nice Leper to Zombie conversion program.

On this particular ramshackled evening, the sky hung low and grim like a moist towlette blanketing the city. As I stepped down from my hog in the Zombie District near an old General Nutrition store, I spotted a couple Zombies rummaging through the tubs of Designer Protein powder. One was pouring a jar of Creatine Monohydrate into his mouth. Since the Creatine was filling his mouth and spilling over his face, I'm guessing he was taking more than the recommended dosage of five grams per day immediately after working out to provide optimum results. I'm guessing, also, that if he did work out, he would probably not gain much muscle anyway. Instead, his arms would fall off. I watched a Zombie struggle to open the lid on a jar of St. John's Wort until he finally just swallowed the entire bottle. The Zombies spotted a dog skulking about the debris, and they managed to corner it against the Amino Force and Blue Thunder weight gain drinks. The dog was snarling and drooling like my ex-wife but was, obviously, less dangerous.

It was time for me to intervene. I came up behind the taller of the two Zombies and yelled, "Hey, Columbo!"

He spun his head all the way around, one eyeball missing. I pimp slapped him with a hefty 1690 edition of the St. James. His entire head sailed across the road and ricocheted off the windshield of a truck that happened to be driving down the street. The side of the truck read "Chicklet Delivery Vehicle." The Zombie head cracked the windshield causing the Chicklet truck to swerve and flip over onto its side. The rear door flew open and thousands of Chicklets spilled out onto the road. The Zombies slipped and fell in the Chicklets. They were sitting ducks.

I went over and cockslapped them into mush with a Gideon. It was then I realized that I'd forgotten to ask them about Bland Entropy.

The Chicklet truck driver clamored out of the truck door (now on top of the sideways truck) and yelled down at me, "Hey! You got your Zombies in my Chicklets!" I grabbed a Zombie by its hair and yanked its head up to reveal its face which was embedded with Chicklets.

"You got your Chicklets in my Zombies!" I responded.

He jumped down and plucked a Chicklet out of the Zombie's face and popped it in his mouth. He munched contemplatively. "Hmmh! That's good!" he finally said.

We got out a meat grinder and ground up all the Zombies and used a heroin needle stolen from a crack junkie to inject all the Chicklets with Zombie meat. We heartily shook hands, and the driver gave me his business card:

Chick Korea

Antidisestablishmentarian
&
Gator Fondler

(pgr) 999-111-9999

"I've got a side business in gator fondling so give me a call if you ever have a need," he explained.

"I certainly will, but...listen...I'm looking for this guy, Bland Entropy. You don't happen to know where I could find him do you?" I asked.

Chick crossed his arms. "Well, I don't rightly know, but I can only suggest you think about this," he said, waving his finger at my face. "If you were him, where would you go? Huh? If you were him, where would you go? Pretty good, huh? From a goddamn Chicklet delivery driver, huh? Ah, fuck off." Then he began reloading his truck.

Looked like the Zombies were a dead end. But Chick gave me a thought. If I were Bland Entropy, where would I go? Where would I go...I knew exactly where I'd go. To the Special Olympics.

Allow me to explain. When I was young I developed a tremendous hatred for the regular Olympics because I had a shot at competing but someone (I'll never know who) fucked it up for me. I was 19 and looking for work. My best friend Catsloser Babyteeth decided that if we got into the Olympics we could earn a living for the rest of our lives getting our faces on the covers of Wheaties boxes. We tried out for the American Feces Throwing team and made it. Things were going swimmingly until that fateful day. I don't know who had the bright idea to hold our practice in the Industrial Fan Outlet. I was busy attempting the Colostomy Bag Squirt for distance when someone accidentally hit a switch and turned on all the fans. You can imagine the chaos. Sudden panic ruined my form, and I threw out my back. Literally. My back is now on a shelf in a closet at home. I only have a front. This comes in handy because it makes it difficult for people to sneak up behind me. However, they can still see my legs from behind, so it's not 100% foolproof.

Ever since our failure to get into the regular Olympics, I've gone to the Special Olympics instead. I pretend to have some physical disability to get in and then clean up pretty much all the awards. I'm special too, dammit, and nobody can tell me otherwise.

Since I like going to the Special Olympics, I knew that if I were Bland Entropy, I'd be on my way to the Special Olympics. So I caught the bus down to, oh, let's say, Atlanta and scammed my way into the competition. I won thirty-seven gold medals including the fifty yard dash for those without hips and the archery tournament for the direction-ally challenged. Well, at least I think I won that one. Most of the judges had been killed by stray arrows.

After my crushing victories, I thought...if I were Bland Entropy, where would I go now? Well...I'm hungry...so, I'd probably get something to eat at my favorite restaurant. Look out Bland Entropy, here I come.

I took the train back to New York and headed to my favorite deli, Fartzy's Delicatessen at the intersection of 5th Street and 7th Road. If I were Bland Entropy, I'd definitely get the cherry blintzes and a knish. A blintz knish combo always put me in the perfect mood for investigation. The owner of the restaurant, Ruben Fartzy, was a nice old coot who worked the counter himself. I tied my pig up outside and walked in. The door jangled as I opened it.

"Mister Donut. How ya' doin' today?"

"Fine Ruben. Just a typical day. Beating up cops and having sex with prostitutes."

"Good for you, Mister Donut."

"Say Ruben," I asked him, looking at the wares behind the counter, "How did you ever end up owning a deli? Did you ever consider toad-licking?"

"Sure, Mr. Donut, everyone thinks about toad-licking as a

career once in their life, but I realized long ago that running a deli is one of the few careers that can satisfy the average heighted individual."

"I hear you, Fartzy. I'll have my usual, hold the placenta garnish, and a slice of that banana nut bread. And, you know what, I'll have some corn on the cob, too. I'm really starving."

"Coming right up."

In just a couple hours, my food was ready. "Hey, these aren't nuts!" I exclaimed after taking a bite from the banana nut bread.

"Sure they are. Monkey's nuts."

"Oh...well, take it back. I'm vegetarian."

I took the rest of my meal and sat at one of the small tables. Unfortunately, I couldn't even balance my plate on it. I hate the fact that Fartzy furnishes the place with dollhouse furniture. I inevitably crush something and have to pay for it. I decided to crouch in the corner, instead, and eat with the plate on my lap.

I was mid-knish when the door jangled interrupting my reverie on Paul Revere who happens to be my favorite patriot. Two men entered, blotting out the light behind them. Dressed all in black, with dark hats, long ringletted hair, beards, and big black shoes. It was...The Orthodox.

They swaggered in cockily, checking the place out, crush-ing doll tables and chairs.

"Hey, watch it! Watch it!" yelled Ruben.

They ignored him. One of them spotted me crouched in the corner. He fixed me with his steady glare. "Have you been Bar Mitzvah'd?"

"No."

"Then beat it," he threatened.

"I'll be in the bathroom if you need me," I told him.

I'm sure I could've taken these two rabbis if I'd wanted to, but I was more curious to find out what they were up to. I made my way to the back, to the bathroom, but kept the door cracked to spy on this Davening Duo while munching on my knish.

They finally stopped wandering about and confronted Ruben. The shorter one spoke, "Listen up, Fartzy. We've got a shipment of under-the-counter lox coming in, and we need a buyer."

"Never. I'll never touch your lox. It'd be unkosher."

The taller one leaned in. "Fartzy, this can be mutually beneficial. We can move your bagels across state lines."

"That means bupkis. I already have a deal with the mimes."

"All right Mr. Wisenheimer," said the tall one as he abruptly pulled a Torah from under his coat and whacked Ruben upside the head with it. Ruben went down like a guy struck upside the head with Moses' tablets.

The taller one began screaming as he swung the Torah wildly, smashing glass display cases and sweeping the counter clean.

"Why is this night more special than all other nights, fuckface?" Gefilte fish flying.

"Part this Red Sea, shit head." Borscht splattering.

"Right here's your shank bone, cocksucker." Pastrami sailing end over end.

Meanwhile, the shorter rabbi had climbed over the counter and was shoving something in Ruben's mouth. "Don't make us circumcise you again, Fartzy. We'll be back." One rabbi turned to the other and said, "We've got to get those mimes," as they stormed out.

I took a piss and then came out to examine the scene. The first thing I noted was that I'd forgotten to eat my corn on the cob, so I stuck that in my pocket for later. The second thing I noticed was Ruben lying on the ground behind the counter unconscious and bloody but breathing. I opened his mouth. Inside...a mezuzah: their calling card. Hmmmh. If I can find these suspicious Hebrites, they could lead me to the mimes. My hunches had been right all along. I reached for the phone to call an ambulance, but it rang just as I touched it.

"Hello, Fartzy's Deli," I answered.

"Satan, is that you?"

"Yes."

"Satan, it's your mother."

"I know who it is Mom, but I have to call an ambulance right now."

"Hold on a second there Mr. In-Such-A-Hurry-He-Can't-Talk-To-His-Mother. We just got back from church, and I need to tell you about the Comedy Cabaret."

"That's nice, Mom."

"The Comedy Cabaret, it was, oh, it was just great. There was the magician-comedian. And his patter was, his patter was just really good. He did the balloons."

"Not the balloons, Mom."

"Well, the balloons. He did the heart with the arrow through it but only as prizes, thank-yous. He really got people to participate. His patter was just great. He did this trick with a woman, and he had done just before that these other tricks with these guys and after the trick, he said, 'Okay, which of these prizes do you want?' and he held up the men's three watches! They didn't even know! And they went, 'Uh, oh, that's my watch.' Then there was an impressionist who did impressions with music so there was a lot of turning on and turning off of the tape player. He did Nat King Cole and his daughter Natalie, an alternating duet."

"Yeah."

"Yes. Then there was a comedian who opened up for Alan King and others. But everyone thought that the magician was the best even though he got paid the least. They did it as a fund-raiser, but as a fund-raiser to get people to come out, but as a fund-raiser we made $4000 for the church."

"That's great, Mom, but have you ever heard anything about a Jewish Mafia?"

"Jewish Mafia, Jewish Mafia. Let me see. Dad! Get on the phone, Dad! Let me think."

Another line clicks.

"What! What you yelling for, I'm not deaf," shouted my father.

"Listen deafy, sure, I just never talk loud enough, right?"

"You mumble."

"Sure, sure I do. Listen our babushka here wants to know if we've ever run into a Jewish Mafia."

"Oh...oh...of course, the Jewish Mafia. No, never."

"What about that time those two rabbis – you told me about this years ago – came busting into your office and one of them had a gunshot wound."

"Wait a minute. There was this one time, years ago, when these two rabbis came stumbling into my office and one of them had a gunshot wound."

"Hmmph," went my mother.

"Do you remember their names?" I asked.

"No, but they called themselves the Hebraic Hitmen. Anyways, I tried to explain I was only a veterinarian, but they insisted so I did the best I could to remove the bullet and patch him up. I remember he was very well behaved through the operation. He never tried to bite me once so I gave him a doggie treat."

"Hebraic Hitmen...that's great info. Thanks, I'll talk to you later."

I hung up on them and dialed 911."You should send an ambulance," I looked down, "oops, I mean a hearse to Fartzy's Deli on 5th and 7th."

I hung up and wiped my prints off the phone then left quickly.

One clue I still needed to follow up on was this Custard Nipplewait character. She was poorly written but extremely intriguing. I looked her name up in a phonebook and found her address on the lower-upper north-south side. I jumped on my hog. Time to roll.

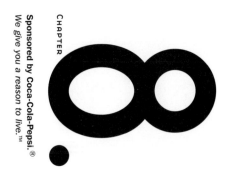

CHAPTER

To: Ratat@calm.com (Satan Donut)
From: Joydivision@dot.com (Etta Donut)
Subject: Once bitten, bite harder

Every guy is either rich little or dick little.

I'm glad you're turning to Andy Gibb for inspiration.
One can never aim too high.

I think I'm really falling for Rodent. I don't want to,
but I can't help it. Tonight after practice, we went
back to my place, and I let him fuck me in the ass. If
that's not true love, I don't know what is. I was in
such a good mood afterwards, I wrote another song called

Grand Canyon:
Everything is fine.
I've got a lot to be happy about.
I've got a husband named George, three kids, a car and
a dog.
But I think there's a piece of my jigsaw puzzle missing.
It's a piece right by the clown's nose.
Everything is fine.
I've got a lot to be happy about.
I've got a kid and a couple of husbands, 2 cats and a car.
We pile the two kids in the car and take a vacation to
the Grand Canyon.
We drive straight through to save time.
I remember no time.
I remember no time stranger.
My husband takes our kid for a donkey ride and
I head up the path for a view.
Now I'm hanging out on a ledge,
Swinging out over a great big Nothing.
Except it might be everything.
I remember no time.
I remember no time stranger.
I don't know what drives me to the edge
except maybe there's nowhere left to go.
I remember no time.
I remember no time stranger.
And I can hear the echo as I let myself go.
As I let myself go.

I know what you're gonna say, but that's what love does to me.

———————

To: Joydivision@dot.com (Etta Donut)
From: Ratat@calm.com (Satan Donut)
Subject: Too loose lat rack

Regarding Andy Gibb, I listen to his albums not because I like his music, but because I have fond memories of when we were lovers. Oh did we love. We loved by the drainage ditch. By the persimmon tree. By the Thames. By the by. Bye bye birdie. Badminton (that's why they call it shuttlecock, eh?)

Listen, I know it's a lot to ask, but I could use your help. My faithful assistant Jenny Sayqua seems to be a bit too busy to help me out right now, and I might need back-up dealing with some ornery characters. Meet me in Chapter 9.

- Malcolm X-Files

CHAPTER

Sponsored by the Republican-Democratic party.
Working together to give you no choices.™

I arrived at Custard's apartment building, tied my pig to a lamppost, and made my way into the building. Behind the front desk was a security guard whose nametag identified him as "Jimmy." I took out the corn on the cob I had in my pocket and struck him on the head with it. The cob broke, but he went down like a ton of bricks. Jimmy cracked corn, and I don't care.

I made my way past him to the elevators and took one up to the fifth floor to room 501. I knocked on the door, and, when there was no answer, I gently opened the door with my mini-jackhammer. I stepped over the remaining shards and jagged splinters into a compact studio apartment. The place may have been small, but it showed a lot of character.

Custard must've been in a hurry because she had left on the TV. Currently playing was an ABC After School Special featuring Scotty Baio. I searched the room and made the following notes:

Object	Qualities	Special notes
Battleship game	unfinished	examined closely. B6 would've sunk her battleship.
Cabbage Patch Kid ashtray	pink	contained cigarettes. Upon testing cigarettes – they taste chalky.
Dynamite magazines	cover feature: "The Hardy Boys: A Dynamite Detective Story" with Sean Cassidy and Parker Stevenson	Look at them – so innocent. who knew that in later years, Sean Cassidy would begin dressing all in black and going to Goth Clubs (all Siouxee and the Banshees with himself) until he joined a cult that worshipped tomato paste and got his head stuck in a drill press. or, even worse, that Parker Stevenson would marry Kirstie Ally, former co-star of the long-running hit Cheers, who would embarrass herself profusely on

Object	Qualities	Special notes
		the Emmy awards when she was jacked on methamphetamines, pulled out an Uzi much like Scarface, and mowed down every single beloved TV star from the early 90's including the stars of Friends. It was so embarrassing it was many years before she landed another TV series. Also found, Bananas and Pizzazz.
Epilady	pink	works on tough beards, too, I discovered.
Fart Powder	white granular material, really smells like farts when pinched	memo to self: don't ever confuse Fart Powder with cocaine again.
Gauchos	corduroy	might be my size. confiscate.
Handcuffs	attached to bed post	who did she apprehend? how did they get away?

Object	*Qualities*	*Special notes*
invisible dog	found leash with stiff wire running along it leading to a stiff open collar. deduced existence of invisible dog at end of leash.	Hold dog for questioning later.
Jelly Bellys	gourmet jelly beans in glass jar	sampled one. mmmh. Coconut.
K-Tel collections	one collection entitled Radical Rock features Alice Cooper, the Captain & Tennille, Paul Anka, KC and the Sunshine Band and Ronnie James Dio	her entire record collection was of this nature.
lunchbox	Annie Sprinkle pictured on side	remember to attend annual Sluts and Goddesses parent-teacher meeting. also, remember to have kid someday.
macramé plant holder	made from macramé	no plant inside

Object	Qualities	Special notes
Naugahyde doll	looks like an owl with big sharp teeth.	ripped stuffing out of doll, but found nothing. Note: beware of owls. They are dangerous.
Operation game	excellent learning tool for doctors to-be	it takes a steady hand
pogo stick	jammed	
Quaaludes	taste like Sour Babies	
rub-on tattoos	taste like ink	
soft toilet seat cover	on toilet	Aarrgh, me mateys, arrgh.
Ty-D-Bol	tastes like Gatorade	
Underoos	featuring Wonder Woman	I determined they are, in fact, underwear that's fun to wear.
Viewmaster	red	disk inside featured the Wonder Twins. Viewmaster was broken. Wonder Twin Powers...unactivated.

Object	Qualities	Special notes
Weird Al Yankovic	curly brown hair, glasses, cheesy mustache	he was sitting there quietly eating toast
X-Ray Gogs	sit my punk ass down, bitch	Note: look up Gogs in dictionary when I get home.
a Yes & Know Invisible Ink Quiz & Gamebook for Ages 12-112.	has yellow invisible ink pen	revealed all answers to see if there was a clue to Custard's whereabouts. nothing.
the collected Zoom! episodes.		

Dammit, I'd searched this place from A to Z and still no clue. Then it came to me, Custard lived in room 732 not 501. I headed up to room 732 and found the door wide open. Her room was in a shambles. I looked down at my feet and saw a small object on the threshold. I bent down and picked it up. A mezuzah. This was the only clue I needed. The Jews got her.

So the Jews kidnapped Custard to try to find the mimes. I had to find those Jews. I would stake them out at the one place I thought they might show up: The Yarmulke Store.

I rode my pig to the Yarmulke store downtown but parked far enough away so as not to offend any Kosher customers. As I entered the store, a series of bells played "If I Were A Rich Man." While browsing, I was soon approached by a salesman.

"Can I help you?"

"Yes," I replied thinking quickly, "I need to buy a fancy Yarmulke as a gift for a bris, but I can't afford more than $11,325.67."

"Not to worry, sir. We've plenty of Yarmulkes in your price range. For example, here's a nice square Yarmulke with gold leaf trim and an embroidered image of Godzilla across the top."

"Perhaps it's a bit dated," I replied. Although the embroidery was excellent.

"Certainly, sir. We have this lovely burgundy keepah made from the laminated skins of old typists."

"Too trendy."

"Very well, sir. Here we have an unquestionably elegant two-story Yarmulke, the first story of finely honed platinum with the entire script of Debbie Does Dallas engraved upon it, and the second story made from ancient redwood with Gila Monster skin stretched tight over it."

"This is lovely," I responded. "How much is it?"

"$10,962.22."

"Oh, also, I have the Yarmulke Discount Card."

"I'm sorry, sir, that's only good for non-sale keepahs. This item is already reduced from $12,269.22."

"All right, I'll take it."

"Would you like it wrapped up?" he asked.

"Actually, no. I think I'll just take it and jam it right up my ass. RRRGHGHGH. Thanks. Boy, I can't wait to shit this out for little Kenny."

The salesman ran away and left me alone. Mission accomplished.

I wandered around the store for an hour or so thinking about a Jerry Seinfeld routine I had once seen about Chanukah. It was really funny. He said something like, "What's the deal with Chanukah? This is supposed to be a holiday? Get this, they only had enough oil to keep the

Temple lights burning for one day...but they lasted eight days instead! What a miracle." Well, he said something like that, but it was funnier. The nice thing about Chanukah is that you can spell it pretty much any way you want: Chanakah, Chanukah, Hanukkah, Hanakah, Hanky, Carcass, Canker, Caracas, Cher, Haricots Vert, Brandon Lee, Tempus Fugit, Pusillanimous, Pustule, Swollen Membrane...whatever.

Finally, the wait paid off. A man entered I recognized as one of the Davening Duo. He went up to the store manager and had a whispered conversation. I tried to listen in but only caught "Shemp Rotenbach Bar Mitzvah." He exited the store, and I quickly followed. He jumped into a car and sped off. He'd spot me on the hog, so I hailed a cab and followed him to a big Marriot Hotel downtown.

I could use a good spanking.

After paying off the cab, I entered the hotel. The hitman was nowhere to be seen, but there was my sister standing next to the entrance with two large plastic bags in her hands. Today she was dressed more formally than usual in black knee-high steel-toe combat boots, skintight black Daisy Duke shorts, and a white bra. Her hair was bright purple with red streaks. I went over and introduced myself.

"I remember you, you're my brother right?" she waved her finger at me.

"That's right. How is your vagina today?"

"It's a bit persnickety," she told me. "It keeps trying to pretend it's a penis. It could use a shoe horn or a talking to or some such."

"What are you doing here?" I asked.

She held up the plastic bags. "I'm supposed to be doing this costume gig with my actor friend Doug Raded. I need the cash, so, what the fuck? He called me up and said they needed a petite girl to do a job with him for $750 bucks so I had to go audition for this woman who hires actors to do costume gigs. So I go to this woman's house, and she's, like, got this massive collection of turkey basters. Like, basters everywhere. Anyways, she asks me to audition for her – to cold read Ophelia from *Hamlet* as if I'm Meryl Streep in *Sophie's Choice* but with an Irish Brogue while wearing a Little Mermaid costume. I basically told her she could either give me the gig or I'd shit all over her carpet. She agreed. What are you doing here?"

"I'm trailing this gangster who's going to a Bar Mitzvah."

"No shit? The Shemp Rotenbach Bar Mitzvah?" she asked.

"That's right," I answered.

"That's whose fuckin' Bar Mitzvah I'm going to," she told me.

"Well, I've got to figure out some way to spy on it." I said, looking around trying to figure out some way to spy on it.

I spotted a sign:

This way to the Rotenbach Bar Mitzvah Reception.

"Since Doug conveniently hasn't shown up, why don't you grab a fuckin' costume, and you can spy that way?"

Hmmmh. It's not a very crazy plan, but it just might work anyway. "Let's do it."

She handed me one of the bags, and I went into the men's room to change. I put on the big head, the tights and black shoes. Looks like I was Mickey Mouse. When I came out of the bathroom, barely getting the head out the door, my sister was standing there also dressed as Mickey Mouse.

"How come we're both dressed as Mickey Mouse?" I asked her.

"Actually, I gave you the wrong costume. You're Minnie Mouse. But no one will know anyway, so it doesn't matter," she explained as she grabbed my gloved hand and led me toward the Rotenbach Bar Mitzvah.

As we walked down the hall, I asked her what we were supposed to do.

We came to the doors of the hall where the Bar Mitzvah reception was being held. "We just stand by the door and give toys to kids as they come in. We're mainly supposed to occupy the younger kids." She pointed at a table with tee shirts, Frisbees, and other junk.

"By the way, it's good to see you...dressed as a girl."

I poked her in her giant eye for that. Then a herd of screeching little kids came running up to us. They circled around us, and one little boy looked up to me and said, "Who are you supposed to be?"

"I'm Minnie Mouse!" I said in a high squeaky voice.

"You're fuckin' gay!" the kid said, and then they all laughed. Some kid kicked me in the side and something bounced off my big plastic head. Due to my limited range of vision, by the time I ponderously turned to see who did it, they were gone.

"Son-of-a-bitch," I said while Etta laughed at me. I tried to grab the kids, but they were quick. Soon a bunch of adults came up, and I had to let go of this one kid I was trying to strangle.

I kept my eyes peeled for the hitman, but he was nowhere in sight. This old guy, about seventy, came up and said, "Cute costume." I felt a pinch on my left breast. I tried to take a swing at him, but he was already gone.

"Calm down," said Etta, laughing.

A couple of thirteen-year-old boys came walking by and laughed at us. "What kind of losers are you?" said this one pimply faced kid before he whacked Etta on her butt.

Etta tried to kick the kid square in the nuts, but the costume restricted her movement. "That's it," she said, "I don't take shit from anyone. I'm going to harpoon that kid right through his anus and out his mouth. I'll drown him in a bucket of hot tar, I'll...wait a second...I got a plan. Follow me."

She led me down the hallway until we happened upon a utility closet. Etta rummaged inside until she came out with some duct tape. Then we headed off to find a kitchen. When we found it, the place was full of waiters and cooks preparing food so I pulled the iM1A2 Abrams Tank out of my pocket. They left quickly. Etta asked me to find two big pots which I targeted by using the onboard RADAR in the tank. Next, we taped the two pots bottom to bottom using the duct tape. We sat the upside down pot over Etta's head and then stretched the neck of her costume so it came up to the lip of the right-side-up pot and taped it there. Then Etta told me to fill the upper pot with Kool-Aid®, ketchup and ground beef which I did. I also tossed in some liver I found for good measure. I put her Mickey head back on over this pot and then led her back out to the party since she now couldn't see. I put the best toy we had – a small slave boy who makes Nike® sneakers from some foreign country which people in the United Stated disregard – into her hands and then led her into the reception hall.

I called all the kids over in my best Minnie squeak, "I'm going to give away the Best Prize to the best little boy or girl!"

"No," said Etta hugging the slave boy to her chest, "I'm going to give it away."

"No, I am!" I yelled back at her.

"I am!" she shouted back at me.

Pretty soon we were screaming at each other, and I tried to grab the slave boy, but she wouldn't let go. A tug of war ensued. "Gimmie that!"

The kids were laughing at us until I started shouting, "You motherfucker! Mickey Mouse is a child molester!" The kids stopped laughing, and I grabbed Mickey's head and ripped it off. Etta swung her head around, flinging meat and ketchup against the walls until she collapsed on the floor in a pool of red. The kids ran screaming and peeing on themselves.

It was then I noticed the Hebraic Hitman. He was hunched over the hors d'eouvres table stuffing his mouth with Kosher weenies like a crack whore at a crack buffet. A kid rolling on the ground having seizures began puking on the

Hitman's shoes. The Hitman finally looked around the room and noticed the chaos. Apparently he decided this was a good time to slip out because he made for the exit. I grabbed Etta, and we stumbled after him. He was heading for the parking lot.

"Did you drive?" I asked her.

"Look for a Vespa Scooter."

"There's no time to lose," I shouted as I pulled her in front of me onto the Scooter which was parked near the entrance. "Drive!"

She kicked it in gear. We leapt onto the sidewalk and then through the front window of the Marriott Hotel. Glass shattered around us as I realized I'd never taken the pots off Etta's head.

"Hard right!" I shouted at her. She jumped the scooter out of the window box and into the main lobby. People were leaping out of our way as Etta turned hard toward the front doors.

"Pop a wheelie!" I barked out. She yanked the front tire up, and the front wheel smashed through the handicapped entrance. We squealed out the door and into the parking lot.

"Sharp left!" We peeled out after the Matzo Murderer. I kept directing Etta until we were one block behind his car.

To make it easier for her to control the scooter, I pulled off Etta's Mickey Mouse costume and tossed the pots away. I was still dressed as Minnie Mouse, but I wasn't about to toss aside a disguise which might come in handy later.

After about 15 minutes it became apparent we were heading toward the bad side of town. I saw Etta's eyes reflected in the sideview mirror.

"You sure you want to follow, Satan? You're a pretty gentile lookin' mouse to me. You might not survive a minute here."

"I'm all right. I just don't want you to risk yourself. Too dangerous. Don't stop the scooter. When we get to the right place, I'll jump off."

"All right, Satan. It's your life," she said.

Etta crouched lower as we began passing burnt out buildings. Gray, brown, grimy. Shattered glass everywhere. Dirt alleys, crumbling cement. The car we were following pulled over to the side and stopped. Etta slowed to about 20 mph. I jumped off the bike and tucked my body into an Aikido roll. Unfortunately, I didn't account for the large Minnie Mouse head. I kept rolling, overshot the sidewalk, bounced off a telephone pole, through a basketball hoop, and into the left corner pocket. I landed in a crouched position on the balls of my feet. I quickly jumped up because it's painful to stand on your balls. If you have balls, you know what I'm talking about. If you don't have balls, then it might be like stepping on your clitoris. If you have neither balls nor clitoris then the world owes you a big apology.

There was a rotting human carcass a few yards away swarming with rats while a single buzzard tore at the remaining flesh. Bare ribs curved upwards like the fingers of a hand clawing at the underside of an ice flow moments before drowning. Welcome to the Jew Hood.

I walked quickly in the direction of the gangster's car and tried to look circumcised. From darkened windows of melted-down tenements, I saw pairs of red feral eyes staring out. These were the wild Jews - half Jew/half badger. They were especially dangerous: they could slit your throat and have you salted and prepared in ten seconds. I hurried on toward the car and saw my mark slip into a non-descript building.

I felt out numbered, skittish. I pulled the multi-level Yamakah out of my ass and pinned it to the top of Minnie's head. This disguise would only fool them for a moment, but sometimes a moment is all you need. I reached the building and read the sign above the door with trepidation, "Rabbi Moshe's Sukkoh." This was without a doubt the roughest bar in Detroit. The bar's motto was "I'm gonna get you, sukkoh." I pushed open the door and stepped into the dingy, gloomy bar.

There were nine guys up by the bar and a single bartender. A bad minyan. The barkeep was seven feet tall with arms as thick and hairy as a grizzly's. He was wearing a sleeveless shirt with the Union Jack on the front. His nose was long and flat, his eyes bulbous and his hands like claws. And the scariest part was, everyone in the bar was cheering because he was being handed a bouquet for first prize in the local beauty contest.

I sidled up to the bar, tucked the yamakah down over Minnie's eyes and tried to look inconspicuous. Eventually, the commotion wound down, and the barguy came my way. He squinted at me suspiciously.

"Mogen David," I said, "on the rocks."

He brought me over the drink. "Fifty."

I waved a thousand dollar bill at him. "I could use a little information." He snatched at the bill, but I pulled it away.

"What kind of information?" he asked.

"I'm looking for a couple characters. Wondering if you could point me in the right direction."

"You mean like Goofy and Pluto?"

"No. I'm looking for a couple of tough guys. Seen 'em swinging Torahs like Sammy Sosa. Mezuzah's their calling card. Some call 'em the Hebraic Hitmen."

The bar suddenly fell silent. Eyes were on me. I heard: click, snikt, chk-chk, tink, Zoinks!, sniff and moo. I recognized the familiar sounds of a pistol being cocked, a switchblade opened, a shotgun reloaded, a cowbell, a rerun of Scooby Doo, and a cow being sniffed.

No one breathed.

I could feel the beam from a laser sight trained on my left synagogue. I mean temple. This could get ugly.

"Who's askin'?" demanded the barman.

"Abraham Rabinawitzenstein."

"And what do you want to talk to them for?"

"You mean, 'For what do I want to talk to them?'"

"Huh?"

"Never mind. I've got a Chinese laundry job they might be interested in."

"How about, I don't think you're Jewish at all. I wouldn't even believe you were Jewish if your name was Moses and you parted your pubic hair with a single wave," stated the barfly.

"No?"

"I've never been so insulted by a stinky Yamakah in my life!"

"Maybe you don't get out enough," I told him.

"Get him boys!" he roared, pulling a grenade launcher from behind the bar.

This was it. Minnie Mouse was about to get fucked.

Just then, a brick came crashing through the front window and landed on the bar. There was a pink bow around the brick and a note tied to it. The bartender ripped off the note and read, "We've come for the Hitmen....Huh?" Just then the front door shattered, and there stood five really pissed off mimes. Guess they were looking for the Hitmen, too. Never thought I'd have something in common with mimes.

Immediately, bullets were flying, mimes swarming – makeup and blood everywhere. In the ensuing chaos, I snuck through a door behind the bar. It led up a flight of stairs. As I climbed, tearing off my Minnie Mouse costume, I thought the scene I left behind would be great in a movie starring Bruce Willis.

I saw this Bruce Willis movie once. At the time I saw it, I didn't know it was going to be a sequel. I thought that if it did well, they'd make a sequel to it. But then, it turns out, they made a prequel instead. In the prequel, the hero, Medulla Oblong, played by Bruce Willis, fights and kills twelve different monsters and then a big boss villain. The twist is – in each battle, he pulls his groin muscle. Yet he fights on. In the climactic scene, the boss monster actually bites off Bruce's entire groin. But later, as the battle rages, Bruce strikes the monster repeatedly in the back with a telephone pole until it coughs up his groin which he puts on ice to be surgically reattached later.

The big hit original, by contrast, is told entirely from the perspective of Bruce's reattached groin. Most of the story is told in voice over as the screen is filled with the shifting material of Bruce's boxer shorts.

I reached the top of the stairs, entering a small hallway. I heard sounds coming from the first door on the right. I drew my two 10mm automatics and went in guns a-blazing. Unfortunately, it was not Custard Nipplewait and the Mezuzah Murders as I had hoped; it was a Driver's Ed class for gangsters. In front of the class was a chalk board covered with diagrams demonstrating how to drive the wrong way down a one way street, charts showing the proper way to spin out, and graphs measuring speed versus distance when driving off a pier. The teacher stopped mid-sentence, and everyone stared at me.

"Well," I said with annoyance, "don't just sit there. Help me put these things out!" I was referring to my guns which were a-blazing on fire. The worst part was that it was an electrical fire. No one ever remembers what you're supposed to do in cases of electrical fire.

There was much muttering, and it was clearly agreed water was the wrong approach. "That'll just feed the fire," cawed Johnny the Crow-Boy. He was obviously master of the obvious. Ted the Cocaine-Coyote felt that someone should talk to the guns. If they were spoken to gently and kindly, perhaps the fire would extinguish itself. Everyone agreed this was a very thoughtful and innovative approach. Billy Hair-of-the-Dog volunteered to make the attempt.

He came away with first degree burns on his lips and nose.

Everyone agreed this was an unfortunate turn of events. Larry the Interpretive-Dancing-Dwarf brought out some Boysenberry Salve for Bill, and everyone was pleased. A mighty cheer arose and wild dancing commenced. The ensuing frolic became the centerpiece of a worldwide movement in support of nudism. Soon, nude people could be seen everywhere: napping in hallways, caroling at Christmas, standing in lines, changing the oil, skiing at Vale, reinventing the wheel, searching for Mr. Goodbar, jumping to conclusions, suspending disbelief, burning down the house, and dangling participles.

I broke away from the nudist revelry and went down the hall to the next door. I wasn't going to make the same mistake this time, having my pistols set on fire, so I drew my trusty Spud Gun instead and busted in.

There was Custard tied with Tefillin to a chair, and the two hitmen leaning over, forcing gefilte fish down her throat. One of them instinctively snapped his Tallis at me and near-ly decapitated me, missing by inches. I fired off several rounds of potatoes. "Splat, splat," they went, pancaking into the hitmen's faces. I latked them to death.

In the silence after the storm, I saw Custard sagging in her chair yet firm of jaw and unbroken. She might be the ugli-est, dumpiest woman I'd ever seen in my life, but in that moment I knew I was in love with her. But I had to be firm. I had a job to do. And jobs always come before love.

I untied her from the chair. She was weak and could barely walk. I slung her over my shoulder and climbed out the win-dow onto the fire escape. The sound of fighting below was still lively. Now I could hear the sound of Jews, mimes and nudists all getting into it.

I climbed to the ground and set off at a good trot. I ran all the way home. It took about twelve hours, but we did stop at a bar for fries and a Budweiser®. (Budweiser®. The beer of drunks.™)

When I set Custard down in my living room, she seemed revived. She stood up and faced me. There we were, finally, face to face, Custard and Satan. Very close. Only about one inch separated our noses. I inhaled her exhale; I exhaled her inhale.

But it was time to get serious. Time to get to the bottom of this with some intense interrogation. "Tell me, Ms. Nipplewait..."

"Call me Custard," she interrupted.

"All right, Custard. I'm going to get to the bottom of this with some intense interrogation."

"Fire away."

"Where!?!?"

"No, I mean fire away with your questions."

"Righto," I responded. "Question number one, numero uno, le numbre one-y...What is your favorite cheese?"

"Gouda," she replied while contemplatively twisting the hair sprouting from a mole on her chin.

"Have you ever smeared half a pound of cheesecake on yourself?" I asked.

"No."

"Have you ever wanted to?"

"Maybe."

"Have you ever found yourself with an excess of cheese?"

"No."

"Do you retain water?"

"Sometimes."

"What do you charge as a retainer?"

"$10,000."

"Did you ever wear a retainer?"

"Yes."

"Who's your favorite entertainer?"

"Sammy Davis, Jr."

"I love that cat. Could you play 'The Entertainer' on an old stand-up piano?"

"Yes."

"Could you play it blindfolded?"

"Yes."

So I blindfolded her and made her play it. Seventy-two times. But she still wouldn't break. Next, I made her wear slippers and run across a recently waxed hardwood floor holding a bowl of vegan chili with lentils. But before she could spill the beans, I stopped her with a peremptory gesture, a philanthropic gesture and followed that up with an obscene gesture.

"Are you hungry?" I asked.

"A bit."

"Let's not throw good chili after...all."

So we sat down and made a fine meal of it. We only had one spoon between us, and it wasn't even a proper spoon, it was a spork, but we took turns. Soon, we were feeding each other until I dropped the spork on the floor.

"It's okay," I said as I quickly snatched the spork off the floor, "three second rule."

Then she dropped the spork on a pile of manure. She picked it up quickly and said, "Three second rule."

"Unfortunately," I said, "that was 3.1 seconds."

Since we were now out of silverware, I used her hand as a spoon, and she used mine. Then my hand fell in the manure.

"Dammit," I said.

So then I sucked the chili into my mouth and squirted it into hers. She did the same for me. I thought this was a clever spork replacement technique. You might want to try it sometime if you run out of clean sporks. Well, anyway, one thing seemed to lead to another...I'm not quite sure how it happened, but we were soon making out. You know - swapping spit, sucking face, mashing, tongue lashing, stipple squeezing. When she finally fell into my arms exhausted from our tonguey love she breathed throatily, "You taste like chili."

"Baby, I know," I replied. "Don't let it get to you. We must resist each other. We're fire and water, you and I. No, more like fire and gasoline. Or nuclear power and more nuclear power. It would be highly dangerous if we got caught up in each other, eh?" I massaged her corns while I continued, "We might forget the outside world. I'd lose all my friends, and you'd lose your job. Next would be asphyxiation, starvation, overpopulation, murder, incest, car bombings, Bhopal-like chemical disasters and a shortage of Funyons."

Her response: "Perhaps I'm a hopeless romantic, Satan, a dreamer, a fool, an astronaut, a piece of French toast, a zebra-skin cummerbund, perhaps I'm all these things, but it'll take a lot more to frighten me off than that. As long as you are aware that the police (and a subsequent restraining order) are only a phone call away. Besides, I firmly embrace the philosophy of Montaigne: accepting the notion of death, its inevitability, is a liberating experience. Montaigne expands upon this belief by purporting that all fears (risk taking, embarking on new creative projects and so on) stem from a fear of dying. Montaigne advocates living life without a sense of futility, enjoying death as a comfortable truth."

"I see you know your Montaigne. Good man, that Montaigne. Didn't he also invent mayonnaise? And yet I find his philosophy difficult to embrace..." I paused to stroke my chin, take out my Meerschaum, pack it, and light it thoughtfully. "Par exempla, how many times have we considered putting mayo on a sandwich or as a dressing, and then reconsidered out of fear. 'Oh, this salad would be ruined by the mayo,' or 'Too much fat in my roast beef already!' And consider: Are there not many times when our fear would be appropriate? Could you eat a peanut butter and mayo sandwich? A mayo milkshake? Mayo in applesauce? And what if you meet someone you think is really neat but don't know if they reciprocate the feeling? If you just go up to them and ask if you can smear mayonnaise on them – well, you can imagine the consequences if they say 'no.'" I puffed slowly on my pipe. "It boggles the mind."

Custard wrinkled her nose. "I loathe mayo for all its weird eggy attributes. Truly, if a bit of mayo even touches me or GOD FORBID I catch a whiff of it...suffice it to say, I'm not happy, everybody in a five mile radius is not happy, and the people who make mayonnaise reconsider distributing it. So, if you perform certain pagan sexual rites involving smearing mayo, you can leave me right out."

I got a sickened, angry look on my mug. I dashed the ugly mug to the floor where it shattered into approximately a million pieces. Whatever possessed me to buy the Mood-Mug Collection from Marshall Tito-Fields?

"Hah! You think you loathe mayo!" I shouted.

With a nervous twitch, I ripped my shirt open revealing many black ringlets of hair. I rent my chest hair with tense-ly curled fingers and finely wrought pinkie rings. The pinkie rings were accessories, if you will – and, I'm assuming here, you're still reading – to the chest hair ripping process. Nay, more than accessories, they were accentuators. My pinkie rings were alluvial detritus on the way to doom brought on by the child within who rules us nigh unto death.

I continued, explaining the nightmares of childhood, "When I was a kid, we were very poor. We ate nothing but mayonnaise and steam. Sometimes I would cuddle up with a jar of mayonnaise (my only friend) and dream of a better day when I might actually have pants."

"However," and here I emphasized my point by snapping off the stem of my pipe and delivered the remainder of my sen-tence through the pipe stem, "Your egotism seems to know no bounds. Our hooking up meant nothing to me. If I were interested in smearing mayo on someone, it sure wouldn't be you! But what about borscht?"

Luckily for me, this angry diatribe sounded more like "Wheet wheet whoot, wheet, wheet, woot, wheet, woot-tweet, tweet, two woo woowoowoo wheat" coming out of my pipe stem. So Custard couldn't take offense and nobody got choked to death. However, I was so enraged my spleen fell out.

"Ouch."

With my arm stretched out blindly, I stumbled into my Guinea Pig habitrail sending exercise wheels spinning and then into the life size replica of Sonny Bono I use as an end table. Custard caught me as I fell on my side. "It's all right," I said, "This happens sometimes, but I keep on. No rest for the spleenless." I struggled to my feet. "Excuse me while I go swallow a pineapple."

As I made my way to the pineapple bar, I muttered, "This is just so typical. Last week I got into a major tussle with my kidneys. They slipped out and ran for the hills. Finally, a Streetwise vendor helped me corner them at Tiffany's. I ended up smashing most of their displays in the ensuing struggle, but at least my kidneys are back where they belong."

Custard called back to me as I bit into a raw pineapple, "I understand. My liver packed it in a long time ago. It was last spotted in Belize making friends with some monkeys."

"Are you telling me that you've got organ problems, too?"

"Yes."

"When I get really mad, my semicolon swells up to ten times its normal size that can be very painful."

,

"It's weird how much we have in common."

"Like we were meant to be together."

"Such a profound connection could only be caused by an alignment of the stars with Jupiter ascendant, Aires rising, and Jebediah was a bullfrog."

"I love you."

"Strange. I don't love you, but I want to rut like a stallion out to stud."

"You know, I've forgotten which of us was speaking."

"I think if I count lines back, you're Satan and I'm Custard."

"I'll take your word for it."

Then we went to bed and made love like there was no

tomorrow. When tomorrow gave a miss and went straight to the day after tomorrow, we were glad it did. It was phenom-enal sex like I'd never had before. We had wild-dingos-ate my-baby sex, Sleeping-Beauty-in-the-Ice-Capades sex, frozen-in-the-arctic-and-committing-cannibalism sex, Godzilla-versus-the-Smog-Monster sex, I-didn't-know-the human-body-could-do-that-pass-me-the-remote-no-I don't-want-any-more-tea-yes-I-voted-Republican-to hasten-the-end-of-the-world sex, fuck-it-all-fucking fucking-fuck-it-what-the-fucking-fuck sex. Yea! Yea!

At this point of the story, my email buzzer went off. I pulled out my handy Porta-Email Pal®.

CHAPTER

Sponsored by God.
I know, I fucked you over. Whatcha gonna do about it?™

To: Ratat@calm.com (Satan Donut)
From: Joydivision@dot.com (Etta Donut)
Subject: When the suicide hotline hangs up on you

This world makes no goddamn sense. Life is pointless.
Some people are born millionaires, others are born hungry. They suffer and die. Show me where this fucking god
is. How could a good god allow this disgusting, pollu-
tion ridden ball of shit to exist. After the Holocaust.
After black slavery. After Joseph Stalin. After
Hiroshima and Nagasaki. After even one single rape. All
of humanity is indicted. The human animal is not good.
Humans prefer having power over others. If god was really good, he would have put everyone in heaven to begin

with, not this miserable hell. So either god enjoys torturing people, or he doesn't exist. We should all be
dead and wiped clean off this planet. Plus my boyfriend
broke up with me.

You're wondering what was it like?

He frowned at me like a weeping sore,
His lips like bubbles of pus.
I shook my head like a wobbly support beam,
And tried to change the subject like a deviated septum,
But he returned to it like the Macho Man, Randy Savage.
He spoke to me like barbed wire,
"Whatever, like, I met this other chick."
I dropped like a wrecking ball above a hobo's shanty.
He departed like my youth and left the taste of Mercury
in my mouth.
I felt like the Hindenburg, like a target at a firing
range.
I brood like the humidity before a tornado
What do I like now?

I think it's maybe time to commit suicide and take as
many people down with me as I can.

My poor sister. Her pain resonates with my own. I remember
the time when I was 6 years old, and I wanted the Barbie

Dream House. Every Christmas and on my Birthday for the next 3 years, I begged for it. Just the Barbie Dream House. That's all I wanted, nothing else. Finally, Grandma Fecal showed up at Christmas with a big box. I knew, I knew, I knew it was the Barbie Dream House. I couldn't sleep that whole night, so excited. Then I woke up early Christmas day and ran downstairs. I tore open the presents. It was the Barbie Dream Shed. I started screaming and screaming. My mom came down and tried to reassure me, "It's just like a Barbie Dream House, sweetie. Just a little smaller." I yelled back at her, "Why couldn't she spend the extra twenty bucks to get me the fucking Barbie Dream House, the stupid bitch." Man, was I pissed. You know? So, I can relate to my sister's disappointment.

To: Joydivision@dot.com (Etta Donut)
From: Ratat@calm.com (Satan Donut)
Subject: As I lay frying

Listen to me, Etta. I know you are very upset right now, but you are not insignificant in this wide, wide uni-verse where a human being is only one over ten to the googol plex power in size relative to the universe.

You can't see the metaphorest for the trees.

Your actions affect us all. Sure, the world's not a

place where I like to hang my hat, but it is a place. You gotta give it that. Without the world, you wouldn't be able to wear shorts. Not even on your head. And you never know when things are going to turn around. Like, just the other day, I was drilling around my appendix when I discovered a large gold deposit. Now I'm rich! Do you hear me? Rich, I say!

Now this Rodent fella, what you got here is a pile of bad judgment. This guy wouldn't recognize the best punk rock singer in the world if she smashed him in the face with a guitar. Not if she jammed roiling maggots down his throat. Are you taking notes?

Speaking of notes, you shouldn't be wasting a second on this scumbag, you should be making a record. Of your music. Listen, I'll get the vinyl, you get the big squeezy thing with grooves in it, we'll press some vinyl. Then we'll grease some palms, and the next thing you know...boom...bigger than Yanni. Think about it.

-Virus Santanna

CHAPTER

This chapter available for sponsorship in future editions.
Just call 1-800-BITEMEE

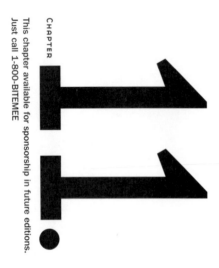

Custard was looking at me suspiciously while I typed my email response to Etta. After I sent it, Custard said. "Who was she?"

"Who she?" I asked back.

"The woman you're exchanging emails with," she replied.

"Are you jealous?" I queried.

"Maybe," she answered.

"Well, don't worry," I reassured her, "it's only my sister. We dated once, but that was a long time ago."

"Oh, all right. It's just...I'm scared."

"I understand," I comforted her. "We're all scared. But you don't have to be afraid. I want to be with you to share this festival we call life, this festivity of lights, this high-falutin' shenanigan, this tempestuous torment, this bitter neglect, this bold interloper, this parochial inhabitant, this antediluvian plebiscite, this paranoid schizophrenic, this Sarasota Minnesota, this hand job, this best of five play-off, this seminal punk band, this punctual coffee maker, this married lesbian, this harried trespasser, this dreary nightingale, and me."

She went on to explain, "I've heard so many excuses, bad break-up lines: 'Sorry, I find you repulsive;' or 'Your urine stinks;' then there was 'I can't meet you tonight because I'm planning to commit suicide.' One guy used a break up line on me that was so awful, I had to set him on fire. I'm considering doing a sociological study of break-up lines. It's all about anomie, the breakdown of society, how we fail to relate to each other – like how people email instead of talking to each other."

"It makes sense that your response to a bad break-up line would be to set someone on fire," I responded. "Fire is magical to us because it embodies the passage of time. We can never grasp time because it is invisible, unreachable and continually slipping from our grasp. Do we live in the present? How can we? The present is infinitesimally small. It

141

can't contain human action. We teeter on the brink between our assumed future...where we will be in moments to come...and our memory of the past...where we think we just were. The present doesn't exist in a comprehensible way. Similarly, fire is something we can neither grasp nor touch, yet it has a clear effect just as does the passage of time. In fact, it has a very similar effect...the decay and collapse of life, the acceleration of entropy. Thus when we stand mesmerized by fire, we are actually mesmerized by our own mortality.

"And break-up lines," I continued, "...ah...a signification of death again, the death of a relationship. However, it's even sadder when people go on pretending the thing isn't dead when it's actually been stone cold for a long time. It's like sitting at dinner with your rigor mortised grandmother. As painful as it might be, I've grown to feel that each relationship ended is an opportunity to shed a new skin and grow again. I think it's much harder to grow while in a relationship than out.

"And emails," I went on, "I believe, are merely another generation's version of letter writing. You may recall the epistolary novel of the 18th and 19th century. Indeed, many friendships and love affairs were carried on through letter writing. *Clarissa* is one example. *Pride and Prejudice* showed how powerful can be the emotional effect of a letter. I would say the collapse of our generation is not due to technology per se, but rather to increased instability of the economy and increased demands of working hours. The insatiable need for profit at the expense of pleasure. I'm actually working on a novel of emails that is entitled *Shakespeare's Day.*

"In Shakespeare's day," I explained, "as you probably know, theater was the most popular form of entertainment. Second only to bear sex. My novel has nothing to do with Shakespeare, I just think it's a profound sounding title which will sell a lot of books. On second thought, maybe Shakespeare will be mentioned tangentially, as a reference in passing. One character might write in an email, 'But, in Shakespeare's day, they didn't have all the modern conveniences we take for granted today like electricity, running water, toilet paper, can openers, bottled water, breast implants, and gerunds. And yet he managed to write a few decent plays and probably had a good time. I mean – how could you be bored when everywhere you go, it's like a Renaissance Fair?' Then the rest of the book will be about cranberry muffins.

"It's a love story set in the South between a cop named Zeke and a donut ho' named Sunny, born out of breadlock. Sure, she done kin before, but that do nut mean she's inbred. When they first meet, Zeke finds Sunny dozen on the side of the road. She's sugar high with a bunch of white powder up her nose. Zeke says he won't arrest her if she'll let him eat her out, but she tells Zeke to bake off. He crumbles, realizing he was cruller than necessary and splits. Sunny knows she's frittering her life away as a prostitute, but she's in debt, so she borrows money from this stuffed shirt from Boston. He plays a critical roll in the story's progress. A member of a secret brotherhood of dunks who study the significance of Apple Pi, this guy sprinkles sweet Sunny with gifts. Even so, his motives are as clear as a greasy paper bag. When he finally gets fresh with her, she's in quite a jam. Sunny is falling apart, she's fried. In a dunkin' rage, she pastes one upside the over-starched Bostonite's head. He pulls a gun and shoots Sunny, but the bullet glazes off her forehead and puts a hole through her stomach. Finally Zeke arrives. The cream puff from Boston is bageling for his life when Zeke crushes him. By the end of the story, Zeke is rolling in dough, marries Sunny, and takes her away to a life of full fill-ment."

Just then I noticed my dog, Bilabial, was crapping on the carpet so I suggested we take him for a walk. As we left my house, Custard said, "I forgot to mention that I know where Bland is hiding."

"That might be helpful information," I told her as we strolled down the sidewalk.

"He has an underground top-secret lair. The main entrance is behind the Égoïste® counter at Nordstroms."

"Égoïste®, that's a cologne right?" I asked her, waving to my neighbor Antonio DiMarco Denada Delusio Grenada Fructose who gave me a funny look.

"Sounds like a breakfast food," Custard noted.

"Recent studies indicate it's as nutritious as Cap'n Crunch® cereal," I explained while my dog peed on a fireman. Hey, if you're so busy putting out a fire that you don't notice a dog peeing on you, that's your problem.

"Fascinating."

We jogged around the block a couple times to give my dog some exercise.

"Well, I better get to work and head to the underground lair."

"Just be careful. I'm probably going to fall in love with you later."

"Okay, I will."

So then I went home and got dressed because we'd been walking the dog in the nude.

I rode my hog to Nordstroms and entered the perfume section. Time to run the gauntlet. Over-made-up counter employees and roving pseudomodels attempting to spray you with colognes, perfumes, exfoliants, detanglers, clarifiers, penis growth serum and fat melters. I made it three aisles before a deathly pale Aramis scout nailed me with a spritz of Tuscany. Goddammit, I could lose an eye that way.

I pulled out my AK-47 and sprayed it everywhere, clearing the entire floor. It took fifteen minutes, glass shattering, blood, guts, perfume, what have you. There was no time to mess around. I crunched over broken glass to the Égoïste® counter.

The body of some guy with an unnatural tan and a bullet hole in the forehead was slumped over the counter. I shoved him off and clambered over. I opened one of the drawers behind the counter, and it revealed a small tray with several colognes on it. I tried one and found it a tad too musky for my taste. I yanked out a shelf, and a secret door opened in the back. I crawled forward into the crawl space. The cement quickly turned to stone as I continued creeping over creepy crawly creatures and crawdads who dawdled along attempting to delay my descent. I licked some lichen to lift my spirits and steady my resolve.

The tunnel leveled out and began to widen. Then it got taller and started putting on weight. As I continued, it lost its hair and eventually became impotent. I came to a large iron door carved with dramatic tableau. I looked closely to see immortalizations of scenes from *The Facts of Life*. One scene where Tootie was roller-skating into the kitchen while Jo had Blair in a headlock and was slicing her throat with a meathook. These were probably outtakes.

I found a small window in the center of the door and rapped on it. The window slid sideways, and a pair of eyes was behind it and a pair of socks. Quickly I demanded, "What's the password?"

"Uh," he stammered, "'Today is sponsored by the letter "M."'"

"All right," I replied, "You can come through."

He closed the window, and I heard a series of clangs, clicks and chains rattling. The door swung open and a ten-foot tall guard stepped through.

"Move along, move along," I commanded.

He said, "Thank you," and started down the hall.

I slipped through the door, pulled it shut behind me, and threw the deadbolt. There was a banging on the window. I slid the window open, and there was the guard.

"Hey, let me in," he demanded.

"What's the password?" I asked.

"'Today is sponsored by the letter "M."'"

"No, I'm afraid that's the password to get *out* of the Secret

Hideout. They didn't tell you the password to get *in* to the Secret Hideout?" I asked him.

"No."

"Then, I'm sorry," I said, "but I can't let you in without the proper password. If you wait a couple months and try again, your password may work. We do recycle passwords on a regular basis. That's the best I can do for you."

"All right," he replied, "thanks for trying."

"No problem."

I shut the window and proceeded down the hall, holding tight to the wall and keeping to the shadows. I came to a wooden door and listened; there was a humming sound coming from the other side. Quietly opening the door revealed another short, dim hallway leading into a larger, brightly lit room beyond. I slunk down the hall and saw in the middle of the room a large machine. The machine, shaped like an eggbeater, sat on a platform surrounded by a metal railing. There were many complicated wires, circuits and metal tubes running in and around it. It was the kind of eggbeater that could beat some mighty big eggs. Perhaps Bland Entropy's plan was to egg the houses of the world! As I approached cautiously, the already loud humming increased in volume. This monstrous eggbeater was no friend to humanity, was it? My throat constricted as I confronted something clearly evil. I felt myself closing in on the end. Could it be Satan Donut's last hayride? There was nothing left to say. Death had called my name. Or maybe it's just. The end of. The paragraph. Yes.

I went up to the railing to examine the device. Hanging from the railing was a clear round globe with a high denomination dollar bill inside. I applied the old eyesight trick called "looking" and saw that it was a thousand dollar bill. There was a hole in one side of the clear globe; the bill was just sitting there.

I looked around. No one in sight. I reached in and grabbed the bill, but then I couldn't get my fist out of the hole. I yanked it, but the ball was chained to the railing and then an alarm went off. I put all my weight into it and pulled. No dice. What a fiendish trap! Four men wearing white makeup and black clothes came bursting through the door and surrounded me. I tried to turn my (lack of) back on them to hide, but it was no use - they knew my hand was trapped. They clubbed me senseless. Well, that was one way to get my hand out.

The next thing I knew, I was in a small stone room with a stone bench. I was handcuffed and hobbled by leg chains. And worse than that, they were piping in music: Zamfir, Master of the Pan-Flute. I had no idea how long I had been out. A metal door slid open and in walked a man whom I was certain was the one and only Bland Entropy. "I'm John," he said. "Bland is right behind me."

So we waited awhile. John scratched his foot in the dust. "Right behind me," he said again. Then he whistled a little unmelodious tune while checking his fingernails. He sighed loudly. "Any second now," he explained. About fifteen minutes passed.

Then another man walked in who looked like Dick Van Patten from *Eight is Enough* if he were a foot taller and Asian. He spoke, "I am Bland Entropy, but I'm in disguise as Bland Entropy. It's a sort of reverse psychology disguise because no one would ever think I would be so stupid as to disguise myself as myself."

At last. Here I was face to face with Bland Entropy, the man of the hour. His eyes were glazed over like Jelly Donuts. He was obviously high on something.

"Satan Donut, I presume?" he asked.

"And you are Bland Entropy," I replied.

"Touché."

"Your ché's...always traveling in pairs," I pointed out.

"I hope you've been treated well, Mr. Donut."

"I've only got one complaint. I'm locked in a small room. And Zamfir blows. Okay, that's two complaints, but once you start complaining, it's hard to stop."

Bland coughed and considered me. "You've been on my trail for a while."

"That's true. Your wife hired me to find you."

"How kind of her," he said sarcastically.

"She needs more money."

"Of course she does. She won't be getting it from me. I've invested all my money in my secret hideout, my mime troops and my special Blattella-germanica-sapiens Converto Raygun."

"Ah! So that's who those guys were in white makeup who grabbed me."

"Correct. Shall I tell you what the Raygun you saw is for?" he asked.

"You shall."

He sucked on his thumb contemplatively, popped it out of his mouth and stared at is as though it were a piece of sushi made of plastic. Then he spoke. "I've been studying weather patterns for many years." His eyes drilled into me with an intensity I had only seen before in the eyes of rabbits being experimented upon by the Gillette Corporation. "Specifically focusing on global climate change. As I'm sure you realize, the burning of coal, natural gas and gasoline results in the emission of carbon dioxide which acts like the glass covering a greenhouse in our atmosphere, letting sunlight in but not letting heat escape. As a result, the planet is warming. Records of daily temperature have been kept for over 120 years and that temperature has increased steadily since 1880, the time of the industrial revolution. The fifteen warmest years on record have occurred since 1980. The Zero Decade was the warmest decade ever. 1995 was the second most active hurricane season and 2004 was the most active season of all time. Don't we all remember where we were when the Tornado Salvador picked up the Statue of Liberty and dropped it on Strom Thurmond?"

I nodded. "He never would have died otherwise."

Bland paced back and forth as he went on, "Total worldwide precipitation has increased during the past century. In some places, as much as fifty percent. In the U.S., the total rainfall has increased ten percent and the number of blizzards and heavy downpours has increased twenty percent with a notable jump in the last several decades. In the past decade, there have been twelve times as many catastrophic floods worldwide as there had been in the previous decade. Before industrialization, the amount of carbon dioxide in the atmosphere was about 280 parts per million by volume. Today it is about 400 parts per million, and I predict it will reach 600 parts per million in two years causing a warming of the planet by 3.5 degrees Celsius. I predict in ten years, we'll all fry like bacon on a skillet."

"Well," I said, "as long as we still have television, I don't care."

"We won't have television because everyone who runs television will be boiled like eggs."

"Dammit!" I jumped to my feet. "We've got to do something about this! How can we save television?"

"It's simple, my friend," he replied. He walked around me in a circle and then began an elegant pas de deux with an imaginary partner. "My other area of expertise," he continued, "is insects. I've been performing thorough experiments on numerous species, and I have discovered, as you might guess, that the Blattella germanica, the common cockroach, is the hardiest of insects in its ability to survive temperature change. At temperatures that will kill humans, cockroaches can relax in comfort with an iced tea. I've evaluated their genetic structure as well as compiling all studies of human genetics and have invented the Blattella-germanica-sapiens Converto Raygun which alters the genetic code of an individual until it matches that of a cockroach."

"You mean..." I started.

"That's right..." he interrupted.

"It toasts bread perfectly every time," I finished.

"NO! It turns people into giant cockroaches so they can survive the coming Apocalypse."

"Oh. You're mad, Entropy, mad."

He sighed. "Let me tell you a story, Mr. Donut. This story is about a guy named Ted. Ted was a man who had three esophagi. He liked to run and play in the street, and one day, even though he was just kidding around, he put a large Cadillac in a headlock, and it slipped a disc. Then he slipped a tongue to the crossing guard, and she bit him on the shin. Chastened and suffering from lumbago, he drove his Winnebago to Togo where he changed his name to Bungie Chord and took up parasailing and making toast. One bright morning his parasail folded up on him, but Bungie was able to glide down using the thermodynamic properties of heat convection to catch some lift off a particularly large piece of toast. The following day, he was arrested for sodomy with a sheep and languished until his 80th birthday in the local hoosegow. Upon turning 80, he invented faster-than-light travel, but, just to spite everyone, he swallowed the plans and died.

"I think the lesson is obvious," he concluded.

"Well, I have a story for you, too," I replied, not to be outdone. "My story is entitled The Tale of Sphincter Boy.

"'Help' cried the innocent young fart, 'I'm being sucked into a vacuum cleaner.' Not to fear. Here comes the grand Sphincter Boy. As Sphincter Boy rolls toward the naive young fart, he extends his pseudopodia and lashes out with unbridled anger at the vacuum cleaner. It was an anger so unbridled even naked horses ran in fear, the foamy slaver splashing off their lips like so much semen on the tip of a penis. Unfortunately, the horses trampled Sphincter Boy, and he lost the first letter of his last name. Sphincter oy was so bemused, he accidentally inhaled the virginal young fart. This caused much commotion in the fart family. The mother fart and father fart commoded together repeatedly. This repetition angered numerologist Tab Fididio, who was counting farts and lost track at 55,000,200,201 due to the commotion. In retribution for another fine mess he'd gotten into, Tab vowed he'd turn to less worthwhile pursuits. He stated, 'I, famed numerologist Tab Fididio, vow to piss my life away on something utterly useless in vengeance against those two damn farts that confused me so profusely. I here-by swear that I will drink myself into a constant stupor. I will bite the skin off my lower lip. I'll clean the sidewalks with ear swabbies. I'll straighten all the staples in America. I will vote in presidential elections. Give me time, dammit, more time.'

"Meanwhile, Sphincter oy took his rightful place in the Jewish Home for the Rectally Impaired. The End." I concluded.

"For that, I'm going to have you killed. Good-bye, Mr. Donut."

"Fair enough," I replied to his back as he walked out with John.

Two mime guards entered and dragged me out of the cell. They dragged me by the leg chains down a long hallway, up an elevator, through a banana patch, into an episode of *La Femme Nikita*, over a book by Mark Leyner, before pearls and after swine. Finally we came to a set of large stone doors.

The two guards shoved me through the stone doors, and I stumbled, tripped up by the leg chains, unable to catch my balance due to the handcuffs. I fell heavily on my face. The guards roughly jerked me to my feet, and I heard a tremendous roar. I was in a cavernous amphitheater the size of a football stadium. The tiered stands were packed with thousands of rabid fans, screaming for my blood. Many of them were on gurneys with IVs, others in wheelchairs with gaping head wounds, some had really bad papercuts, but they were all frothing at the mouth shouting, "AB Negative! AB Negative!" Sure enough, my blood type.

The guards goaded me forward with electric anal probes. They walked me down an aisle toward the central raised platform in the middle of the stadium. The ceiling arched high over head, a stone dome with interesting quartz and limestone striation. In the center was the old squared circle. A traditional boxing ring. High above the ring was a scoreboard with large screen TV monitors on each side to provide close-ups of ring action. The guards unlocked my chains and cuffs and then prodded me into the ring. They stood by to make sure I didn't run anywhere. I wasn't about to make a break for it with the threat of an electric anal probe at my rear. At least, I'm pretty sure they were anal probes. They looked like the kind I'd seen before. I mean, if they were regular anal probes, fine, I'd make a break for it. But not the electrical type.

A group of men entered the stadium from the opposite aisle. They formed a circle to keep the crowd away from someone in their midst. I couldn't quite make out what this monkey in the middle looked like as they made their way toward the ring. The crowd's roar rose to a deafening level. This, then, was my opponent. The hometown favorite. The men swarmed like bodyguards into the opposite corner, and I still couldn't see whom I was fighting.

A man in a tuxedo stepped between the ropes and moved center stage. A microphone attached to a long cable dropped from the scoreboard, and the ringmaster took it in his hand. "Ladies and gentlemen! Ladies and gentlemen!" The crowd hushed. "The main event you've all been waiting for! The once biannual no-holds-barred Death Match brought to you by Bland Entropy and Miller Lite® (Miller Lite®. Since it tastes like piss, you can drink it twice.™) In this corner, six feet tall, weighing 210 pounds...the dastardly nimrod Satan Donut." Boos and hisses.

"And in this corner, four feet tall weighing 100 pounds, George." The bodyguard retinue finally parted, and I saw my foe. It was a high-backed Louis the Fourteenth armchair. Thick mahogany wood, a red, elegantly cushioned seat and backrest. The crowd went nuts. I knew, right then, I should have moved to Miami.

A bell rang and the trainers pushed the chair forward to the center of the ring. I circled him warily, but he sat there biding his time. I faked a few jabs, juked left, went right, but George wasn't falling for it. I tried some fancy foot moves, winged a jab, cross, hook combination. I connected with the hook, but George shrugged it off. Practically immune to my punches, he didn't even flinch. His strategy was to tire me out, out last me. I didn't have much choice. I was going to have to go for it, all or nothing.

I dove hands first, stretched full out, straight for him. I managed to get an arm around his back, quickly threw an armlock on him, and took him to the ground. I twisted my hips and put the chair in the traditional Brazilian Jujitsu "guard" position. Then I used the heel of my right foot to pound on one of his legs. If I couldn't take him out with brute force, I'd wear him down. After I felt that I had inflicted a decent amount of damage to his leg, I rotated my hips again to slide on top of him and got him in the Brazilian Jujitsu position known as "The Mount." I held him tightly against my chest so he couldn't strike at my eyes and then began gouging at his cushions. I tore and ripped and shredded like a mad beast until I was down to the bare wood. Then I began gnawing at it like a beaver. I finally pushed off and got to my knees.

There George lay, the stuffing entirely ripped out of him. He looked like a gutted deer. I became aware of the crowd. They were going insane, tearing each other apart, legless people being tossed in the air, IV bags splattering. The microphone came down again, and the host started shouting for order.

The audience began chanting, "Kill him! Kill him!" They stumbled toward the ring menacingly. I knocked the host aside and grabbed the microphone. I shouted, "Eat me, you blood sucking scum!" They surged forward, apparently trying to eat me. I hooked the microphone around my belt then began climbing up the attached cable, bringing the end with me. When I got up to the scoreboard, the crowd was bouncing around like a bunch of Chihuahuas on lava, shaking their fists at me. I gripped about halfway down the cable then leapt off the scoreboard.

I swung out above the crowd as they snapped at me like alligators. I let my grip slide so that I swung the full length of the cable, released, flew over the heads of most of the crowd, landed far down the aisle on top of an old man stretched out on a gurney. He was knocked senseless, and we flew at top speed down the aisle.

I stood up on the gurney, put on my Walkman, popped in a

Dick Dale cassette, and rode down the aisle, out the doors, down a flight of stairs, through a wind tunnel, over a hill, under a dale, to Grandmother's house (I introduced my Grandmother to Babby Babbage - he was the old guy on the gurney with me. They got along famously and ended up getting married in Vegas even though Babby never regained consciousness) to Shelly Duvall's house and finally to Baby Doc Duvalier's grave. I danced on his grave then lay down and ate some dirt for a while. That was fun. Next I went and strangled a Boy Scout. I think he had it coming. A police officer caught me, but I told him I did it because I had bad allergies. He let me go.

Have you ever nude Jello wrestled with really short guys? The reason I ask is that after I strangled the Boy Scout, I became involved in a Skeet shooting accident involving Carmen Electra and Yasmine Bleeth from *Baywatch*. And a couple really short guys. By the way, if you say "Yasmine Bleeth" fifty times really fast, it gives you a head rush.

Did you ever notice how charmingly anachronistic practicing Catholics look on Ash Wednesday? Especially in a corporate environment. Suit, white shirt, tie and big smudge of soot on the forehead. I expect them to pull out a spiked club to bang on their flowcharts. The reason I ask is that the skeet shooting accident took place in the corporate headquarters of The First National NBD Bank One Citibank bank in downtown Boston. Carmen, Yasmine and I were standing between velvet ropes in line waiting to deposit our paychecks.

No, seriously.

And the line was moving very slowly. There were also a couple really short guys in line with us. I've got nothing against really short guys, mind you, but these really short guys were nasty. They began insulting the actresses' talent, saying they'd only been hired for their boobs, and so on. The final straw came when one of the really short guys accused Ms. Electra of not being able to distinguish between the teachings of Stanislavski and his disciple Lee Strasberg. Carmen, you see, is a method actor to the core (and that's actually why she got a breast enlargement – because her character on *Baywatch* would have). Anyway, Carmen and Yasmine hog-tied the really short guys with the velvet ropes and pulled out skeet guns.

They asked me if I would do the honors, so I flung the really short guys in the air using the velvet ropes like a sling shot. Carmen, ever the perfectionist, said that I needed to wait until she yelled "pull." So I had to do it again. I retrieved the now stunned really short guys, wrapped them up and this time waited until she shouted "pull" before I fired them into the air.

Carmen, a keen shot, blew off her really short guy's lips with two quick shots. Yasmine, however, was way off the mark and shot a banker right in the center of his forehead where he had a sooty mark for Ash Wednesday. She wasn't trying to make an anti-Catholic statement or anything, she was just a lousy shot. This was quite embarrassing, and she received a stern reprimand from the police when they finally arrived.

The policeman set up Insta-Judge® from Intel-Microsoft-Apple. Yasmine was tried and found guilty on the spot. They sentenced her to five years remedial skeet shooting classes, but citing her duties on the show *Baywatch*, the Insta-Judge® reduced her sentence to two years occasional Virtua-Cop XIV playing on the Sony-Mitsubishi-Nintendo Playstation.

Well, I finally deposited my check, and I was back on the case. But first I had to nap, so I went home and caught a nice forty-five minutes of zzz's.

When I got up, I realized I hadn't cleaned my kitchen so I immediately set to work with my de-dirtifier spray. I scoured my kitchen counters and discovered a paramecium named Carl who likes rain, long summer walks and dancing 'til dawn. He told me a few jokes that were quite cilia, but the point is that it's better to have a paramecium in front of you than a paramecium in your intestines. However, that might be a fluke.

I abruptly realized I'd forgotten all about Bland Entropy's dastardly plan to turn everyone into cockroaches. I certainly wasn't going to let that happen to someone as valuable to the world as Keanu Reeves, let alone myself, so I immediately headed back to the secret hideout. I ran through the Nordstroms and down the passageway to find the same guard still waiting outside the door for his password to go into effect.

"Still waiting, huh?" I asked.

"Yup."

"Say, you sure got a lot of keys on that keyring attached to your belt," I noted.

"You mean this?" he asked, holding up the thick, iron key ring. "These are just the keys to unlock the door."

"I see. Do you mind if I borrow them for a second?"

"Okay. Just make sure to give them back to me."

I unlocked the massive door's ten locks and returned the keys to him. "Thanks."

"No problem," he replied.

I ran straight for the Cockroach Gun room to dismantle it. I pulled a monkey wrench out of my underwear upon entering the room, but then I noticed they'd changed the thousand dollar bill in the globe to a five thousand dollar bill. I wasn't about to let them make a monkey out of me this time.

I reached in to grab it and set off the alarm again.

DAMMIT! Will I never learn that greed only gets you money?

The mime guards came running in and clamped me in chains again. In walked a woman who looked exactly like Kate Winslett, but when she spoke it was with a deep man's voice. "So we meet again, Satan."

"Bland?"

"That's right." He picked up the monkey wrench now on the floor and twirled it like a cheerleader. "Well, Satan Donut, since you've shown such interest in my machine, I think I'll use you as the first test subject."

"Aw, shoot, can't you wait until you're sure the thing really works? I'd hate to have you try it only to be disappointed."

"My mimes, chain him to the wall."

They put me against a spot on the wall with a bull's-eye painted on it and several protruding hooks to which they tied me.

"I'm really glad you came along. Now I'll find out if my ray needs any tweaks."

"God, I hate the word 'tweaks.'"

"Shut up you idiot!" he yelled.

"Sorry. Just thinking out loud."

"All right." Bland went behind a computer monitor and pressed a few buttons. The large gun swiveled to point directly at me and began pulsing with electricity.

"Any last words, Mr. Donut?"

Before I could reply, a buzzing came from behind the computer panel. Bland pulled a little device out of his pocket and put it to his ear. It was a cell phone.

"Hello?" He listened, then gestured one of his mime guards over, pointed at me and gave the guard the cell phone. "It's for you."

The guard brought the phone over and placed it against my face.

"Hello."

"Satan, it's your mother."

"Mom, I'm about to be turned into a giant cockroach."

"Oh, sure, never a moment for your mother. Never a second. Well, Mr. I'm-About-To-Be-Turned-Into-A-Cockaroach, we had a big trauma today, and I think you need to hear about it."

"Okay Mom, what is it?"

"Well, let me get your father on. He can explain it better than I can. Dad! Dad! It's your son. Come quick, before he turns into a cock-a-roach."

There was a brief pause, then a line picked up.

"Hello."

"Dad."

"Tell your son about what happened today," ordered my mother.

"What, what?" said my father.

My mom explained, "We were driving on the Berlin Turnpike, and your father was in the left hand lane."

"That's right, but I was about to move over to the right hand lane."

"Sure you were. I told him to watch for exit 53 to Newington/Wethersfield, because he always misses it."

"Only because you're distracting me with your harpy cries."

"Sure, sure, Mr. Jason-and-the-Argonauts. So there's this tricky part where two lanes become one. Anyways, as usual, I have to tell him to shift lanes, but it's too late, we miss it. So we're driving along the turnpike, when I notice Lechmere's has closed. And the Whiz. What else?"

"Hmmh?" my father grunted.

"What else closed?"

"The Whiz?"

"I already said that one."

"I didn't know until they had the close-out sale at Lechmere's that it's owned by Montgomery Ward," said my father.

"So anyways, they opened a new restaurant, Piccadilly Park and another one Uncle Joe's. But then Uncle Joe's closed and they opened 99. Since we missed our exit we decided to go to 99 for dinner."

"That's right."

"The salad bar was great, and the pasta is good. But then, here's the thing. Your father almost got food poisoning."

"Mom," I asked, "how does one almost get food poisoning?"

"Well, Mr. How-Does-One-Almost-Get-Food-Poisoning, I'll tell you. Your father had the chicken for dinner. He took one bite of it then said, 'Hmmh. Doesn't taste like chicken.' I smelled it, and it smelled a bit strange. We called the waitress over and pointed out the chicken. She apologized, saying that there must have been some mistake, he was served the raw fetus special. So then your father went and vomited in the bathroom."

"I did."

"Good thing he didn't eat more than that. He would have had food poisoning."

"Okay, Mom. I gotta go. I've got things to turn into."

"All right, boychick."

"Bye son."

They hung up.

I gestured to the mime that the conversation was over, and he returned the phone to Bland. Bland spoke, "I ask you again, Mr. Donut. Any last words?"

Oh, mungy, mungy day. Not even Bartholomew of 500 hats could find a hat to fit this situation. I wanted to say something profound like, 'Love man, love is all there is,' but I was too choked up thinking about the episode of 90210 I saw the other week where Jason Priestly had to have his spinal cord removed because it was sending 1000 volts of electricity coursing through his body every half hour, and he struck Tori Spelling so hard with his flailing limbs that he knocked her head clean off.

My thoughts got all mixed together when I finally spoke, "Have a 90210 Christmas. Myself, I abound in joy for the smallest shit eating creature to the largest except for the human race which sucks. Last Christmas, I only got coal for Christmas, and they were hot coals which burned a hole in my stockings and set fire to my garters. (I usually cross-dress on Christmas in the spirit of the Holy Moly Mother Mary and her all virgin choir who are just looking for a good spanking or a talking to.) Good-bye cruel world."

"Cheer up," said Bland. "Life can only suck once."

He triggered the machine, and a beam of energy fired at me. I quickly brought my legs up into a pike position with 3.5 difficulty and took the shot with the bottom of my feet. Fortunately for me, my shoes are made of ultra-reflective Osmium (the densest element in the universe) which just happens to be perfect for deflecting energy beams from Blattella-germanica-sapiens Converto Rayguns.

I reflected the beam directly back at Bland Entropy. It caught him right in the chest. He began screaming in agony.

I then redirected the beam to catch the two mime guards who opened their mouths wide as if they were screaming, but no sound came out.

The three of them fell to the ground in seizures. They began mutating – their skin burst off, revealing muscles which began crackling and turning black. Their hands turned into claws and their ribs ripped out of their sides growing into additional legs. Pretty soon all three looked like giant cockroaches.

The one that used to be Bland Entropy made loud clicking sounds and charged toward me, but before he could get halfway to me one of the former guard roaches jumped on his back. Blandroach tried to shake him off, but Guardroach was clamped down. He inserted a tube of some kind into Blandroaches thorax and started pumping fluid into him. I think they were having sex. Then Guardroach2 scuttled over and whacked both of them in the head in a rit of fealous jage. Black roach blood began to flow and while the three roaches began snapping at each other, I lockpicked my way out of the chains with a lockpick I had hidden in my ear.

I retrieved my weapon belt tossed on the floor by the guards and pulled a mini-nuke pack (McDonnell-Douglas-Boeing Nukepaks. The best way to rid yourself of unwanted guests.™) and planted it at the base of the Cockroach Gun. I set the timer for ten minutes and ran for it.

I ran down the hall, out the door, by the guard, by the guard, and by the guard. The third time I went by the guard, I realized I was running around him in a circle.

"C'mon," I said to him, "Beat it. There's a nuke about to go off."

We hightailed it out of the hall and up the tunnel and then broke off in different directions. His direction, unfortunately, was back down the tunnel. What can you do?

The nuke went off just as I cleared the threshold distance. There was a huge boom and a gout of earth about the size of a two football fields lifted up in the air and came down in the form of Elizabeth Keller, who is my friend David Katzman's beautiful girlfriend. How ironic that this gorgeous woman would forever stand as a monument to the folly of those who would try and save the human race from destroying itself. Or whatever, dude.

I crossed the town square and turned a corner, and who was waiting there for me but Custard Nipplewait. She was wearing a thin black negligee showing off her goiter hump and turkey neck. She held a jar toward me, her underarm flab swinging gently in the wind.

"I brought the mayo. How 'bout you 'n me get eggy?"

"I caught her in my arms and kissed her bald spot."

● *david david katzman*

"Why did you just say that?"

"Oh, sorry, I meant to do it, not say it."

So I did. It was the perfect ending to a perfect day. And that's how the story ends. I believe its significance is clear. Good night.

Sponsored by Monsanto-Wal-Mart-General Motors-Shell-Phillip Morris-NBC-Mary Kay, Inc.

Owning your soul since 2001.

February 21, 2018

Satan Donut
10 Tom & Dick Hill
Cleveland, OH 00800-6666

Etta Donut
United Nations
1 United Nations Plaza
New York, NY 10021

Dear Satan:

Thanks for including me in your book. As you know, however, it is not appropriate for the U.S. Ambassador to the United Nations to be portrayed as a punk
rock maniac who says, "...we went back to my place, and I let him fuck me in
the ass." Such unsavory details, as well as the mention of an alleged previous
romance between us, will hurt my career in politics. As such, you will find a letter from my lawyer attached. We are suing you for liable and requesting a pro-
hibitory injunction on the distribution "of" "your" "non-fiction" "book" from
Circuit Court Judge Myron P. Whitesgetoff.

Etta Donut

About the Author

David David Katzman is powered by polyester and ancient spaghetti with magical properties. A painter, writer, comic book addict, contemporary art lover and recovering actor, David^2 resides in Chicago with two cool cats and something, something, something. This is his first novel. He can be reached at juxtapozbliss@yahoo.com, and, yes, his first and middle names really are David.